Mills & Boon Sensual Romance® is delighted to bring you this wonderful short story by international bestselling author Kate Hoffmann!

Are you in the mood for a wedding?

Then you'll love this unforgettable trip down the aisle in…

SHE'S THE ONE!

KATE HOFFMANN

Kate began reading romance in 1979 when she picked up a copy of Kathleen Woodiwiss's *Ashes in the Wind.* She read the book from cover to cover in one very long night and was immediately hooked on the genre.

Nearly 10 years later, while working as an advertising copywriter, Kate decided to try writing a romance of her own. After a history of interesting jobs in teaching, retailing, advertising, and non-profit work, she was determined to add romance author to that list.

After numerous failed attempts over three years, Kate decided to forget writing historical romance and turned to category romance. Six months later, her first story, *A Vagabond Heart*, was finished. A year later, Harlequin Mills & Boon bought the book after Kate won a competition. The book was published as *Indecent Exposure*.

Her dream of adding romance writer to her resume came true and in December of 1993 she turned off her alarm clock, shredded her pantyhose and became a full-time writer.

Kate lives in Wisconsin, USA, in a cosy little house in a picturesque village. Two cats also live with her — Tansing, a grumpy Himalayan, and Tibriz, a tortie Persian mix that she rescued from an animal shelter. She enjoys gardening, golf, reading and romantic movies.

Praise for Kate Hoffmann:

'Kate Hoffmann creates a delightful tale that mixes light humour with deep emotions.'
—*www.romantictimes.com*

Kate Hoffmann's latest really is 'sassy, sexy and seductive.'
—*www.theromancereader.com*

'Kate Hoffmann's characters send steam off the paper!'
—*www.romantictimes.com*

DID YOU PURCHASE THIS BOOK WITHOUT A COVER?
If you did, you should be aware it is **stolen property** as it was reported *unsold and destroyed* by a retailer. Neither the author nor the publisher has received any payment for this book.

All the characters in this book have no existence outside the imagination of the author, and have no relation whatsoever to anyone bearing the same name or names. They are not even distantly inspired by any individual known or unknown to the author, and all the incidents are pure invention.

First published in Great Britain 1999. This edition 2004.
by Harlequin Mills & Boon Limited,
Eton House, 18-24 Paradise Road,
Richmond, Surrey TW9 1SR

ISBN 0 263 84110 3

054-0104

Printed and bound in Spain
by Litografia Rosés S.A., Barcelona

SHE'S THE ONE!

by

Kate Hoffmann

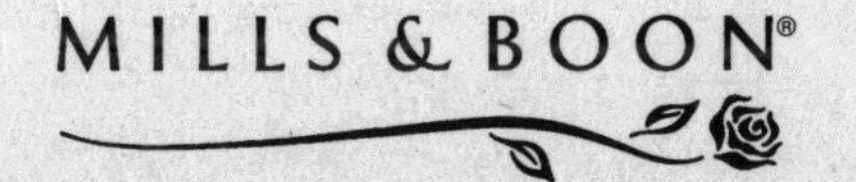

Chapter One

STEEL GRAY CLOUDS SCUDDED across the sky, whipped by a damp wind off the Atlantic. Chase Donnelly leaned against the railing of the porch and stared out at the choppy water, following a whitecap until it dissolved on the sandy beach far below him.

How many times as a boy had he stood in this same spot, on the sprawling veranda of his grandmother's huge Victorian summer house, and stared out at the sea, dreaming of adventures in faraway places? Summerhill had been his second home for as long as he could remember.

He had first come here as a child. On the night before the last day of school, he and his two brothers would pack their bags, stuffing a summer's worth of toys into their duffels, along with a few T-shirts and pairs of shorts. They'd leave for Nana Tonya's the minute school let out, Nana's chauffeur picking them up in the Bentley to make the drive from Boston to Woods Hole.

The summer officially began the moment Winston drove the Bentley onto the car ferry for Martha's Vineyard. Chase would hop out of the back seat and run to the bow, hanging his arms over the gunwales and turning his face into the spray. The tangy sea breeze would seep into his skin and ruffle his hair, and the waves beneath the bow of the ferry would set his body swaying in an instinctive response.

His life in Boston, so staid and proper, would slowly disappear behind him and the summer would rise up ahead—sparkling blue water, white sand dunes and rustling sea grass. Endless sunny days full of adventure in his little sloop, with its sun-bleached sails and wooden mast. Life had never been so good or so right. And he'd wanted it to last forever.

Chase chuckled softly and shook his head. To hear his family tell it, he still lived the summers of his boyhood. According to his father, he'd never grown up. But Charles Donnelly III knew nothing about his eldest son, Charles IV. All his father knew was profits and losses, strategies and maneuvers. He knew the family business more intimately than he knew his own family.

''Daydreaming again?''

Chase turned to find Nana Tonya standing in the doorway, her white hair slipping from the tidy knot at the back of her head and whipping around her gently lined face.

''It won't be long until I can sail over for a visit, Nana. I put the boat in the first of April.''

She slowly approached, leaning heavily on her cane. ''And what then? Will you keep on sailing like you did last summer? And the summer before?'' Chase could still detect traces of her Romanian accent in the pleasant lilt of her voice.

Chase smiled. 'There's a good idea,'' he said.

''Your father wouldn't think so.''

He touched his grandmother on her shoulder. "I'm sorry. This is your birthday party. We're supposed to be one big happy family. The last thing I wanted to do was get into it with Father."

Nana reached out and ran her palm along his cheek. "I expected nothing less," she said.

Chase arched an eyebrow. "That famous second sight of yours hard at work again?" Nana Tonya took great pride in her Gypsy ancestry and her ability to see the future. The rest of the family found it an embarrassment, especially when she talked about her visions so openly. But Chase found it charming.

"Your fights have become a family tradition," Nana said.

"Holidays, birthdays, anniversaries. I provide the entertainment."

Nana shook her head wearily. "You will never be able to make him happy until you settle down and take your rightful place in the family business." She paused and sighed. "And he will never make you happy until he understands the man that you are. With you two, there is never room for compromise."

"So what do you see for me, Nana?" Chase teased. "Tell me my future."

"I don't have answers to your questions, Chase."

"All right, how about stock tips? You've steered me right on more than one occasion. Made me lots of money. I'd even settle for a baseball score. Are the Sox going to win their season opener?"

Nana patted his cheek again, then turned to look out

at the ocean. "You know that my visions are not like television. I cannot turn them on and off at will."

Chase draped his arm around her shoulders and stared out at the horizon with her. "How did you ever find a place in this family, Nana? You and your Gypsy blood marrying into all this stuffy Boston tradition."

"I fell in love with your grandfather and he fell in love with me. I remember when Charles told his family that he wanted to marry me. He was always the rebel, and they thought he'd chosen me because I was so unsuitable. You are a lot like my Charles," she said, a wistful smile touching her lips.

"But you made it work, Nana. You fit in."

"I did it because family was the most important thing in the world to me." She stared at the horizon for a long time, her expression still and serene. Then she suddenly shivered and turned to him, her brow furrowed. "Tonight you will dream of the woman you will marry."

Chase blinked in surprise. His sharp laugh died on the breeze. "Come on, Nana," he chided. "Don't tease."

Nana shrugged. "I have seen it. Just now."

"You're serious?"

"Believe what you will."

"I always take your visions seriously," Chase replied, "because you're always right. But I wanted a stock tip. I'm not looking for a wife."

She slipped her arm through Chase's. "A wife might do you some good, Chase Donnelly." She gave his arm a squeeze. "We must go inside now. Your mother has probably set fire to my birthday cake and I must make a wish and smile about growing another year older.''

They walked back into the house, arm in arm. The cozy dining room grew silent when Chase appeared. The family was still gathered around the table, right where he'd left them fifteen minutes before. Chase's father, two younger brothers and their wives were all in their Sunday best—tailored suits and designer dresses. Always the rebel, Chase had arrived in wrinkled chinos and a faded polo shirt.

''There's the lady of the hour,'' Chase's father cried, jumping up from his spot at the far end of the table. He took his mother's hand and led her to her place at the head of the table, shooting Chase an annoyed glare as he pulled out her chair. ''Maybe now we can act like grown-ups?''

Chase grabbed his napkin from his spot and sat down. ''Oh, let's not. Nana deserves to observe our family in its natural state, don't you think?''

Chase's mother glided into the room with the birthday cake and sent him a warning look. ''Nana, you shouldn't have gone outside without your wrap. You'll catch your death.''

Nana Tonya leaned back in her chair. ''After ninety years, I think I'm capable of taking care of myself, Olivia. Chase and I were having a nice talk.''

''Was he pumping you for stock tips?'' John asked. The middle boy in the trio of brothers was the most like their father—conservative, self-important and cynical. Patrick, the youngest, hadn't yet revealed his true colors. Though he showed a proclivity toward John's character traits, he still occasionally looked to Chase as a role model.

Nana bent closer to the cake and blew out half the candles, leaving the remainder of the task to Olivia. "I told Chase that tonight he would dream of the woman he'd marry."

All eyes at the table turned toward Chase, and he saw a tiny smile quirk the corners of Nana's mouth.

Patrick's jaw dropped. "Chase? Marry? I'd sooner put money on Donnelly Enterprises going bankrupt than on my big brother tying the knot."

Chase shrugged. "What's so hard to believe? You don't think I'd be able to settle down? I'd like to find a woman and get married. I'm no different from any other man." He cursed the defensive tone in his voice, loath to be baited into another argument.

"Sure," John replied. "You'd make a helluva husband, if you could only stay in one place for more than a week and confine yourself to one woman."

"When I meet the right woman, I'll know," Chase muttered. "I just haven't yet."

"I'll be surprised if you can find her in the crowd," John countered.

Olivia pointed at John with the cake knife, clearly aggravated with having to referee another battle within the Donnelly clan. "Boys, this is Nana's night. Can we please just change the subject?" Usually Chase's father stepped in, but he was quietly observing the interchange between his sons.

"You have absolutely no career aspirations," John

continued, ignoring his mother. ''You jump from one thing to another.''

''I don't choose to work in the family business,'' Chase replied. ''But that doesn't mean I don't work.''

''You can't call that import business a career,'' Patrick commented, getting into the spirit of baiting the black sheep. ''How much do you make in a year?''

''He's a cheese salesman,'' John said. ''When he's not sailing around the world and chasing women. How much do you *think* he makes?''

''I have interests in a company that imports wine and gourmet foods, not just cheese,'' Chase said, trying to keep his voice even. ''And do I have to remind you that Great-grandfather Donnelly delivered milk and cheese door-to-door on a handcart when he was a kid? Our family has a long-standing business relationship with cheese.''

''Owning a small import business doesn't come close to running a division of Donnelly Enterprises. When was the last time you set foot in our offices?'' John asked.

''I can't remember the last time I was invited,'' Chase countered.

Chase's father tossed his napkin on the table and stood, cursing softly. ''Well, I'm inviting you now, dammit. You're a stockholder and board member. It's time you took some interest in the business. You'll report to John's office tomorrow morning.''

''Is that an order?'' Chase asked, his jaw tense with suppressed irritation.

Chase's father's expression turned cold. ''Do what

you want. But if you expect to maintain your seat on the board, then I'd suggest you spend a few days a week learning a little more about the family business." With that, he walked out of the room.

An uneasy silence grew at the table, Nana Tonya watching Chase with a curious gaze. As always, John and Patrick's wives pasted polite smiles on their faces, maintaining a safe distance from family squabbles. And Olivia, ever the peacemaker, cleared her throat before she began to slice the birthday cake.

"Why don't we have our cake and coffee in the solarium?" she suggested brightly.

As the family gradually rose from their places, Chase remained in his spot, as did Nana Tonya. A few moments later they were alone in the dining room. He braced his elbows on the table and studied his grandmother shrewdly over his steepled fingers. "Somehow I get the idea that you orchestrated this whole thing."

"Believe what you wish," she said, an enigmatic smile on her lips.

LATER THAT NIGHT, asleep in his old bedroom at Summerhill, surrounded by memories of his childhood, Chase Donnelly dreamed of a woman with hair the color of spun flax and eyes as blue as a Pacific lagoon. She stood on the bow of his sailboat, her flowing white dress fluttering in the breeze, her skin kissed golden by the sun.

She smiled and walked toward him, his name like a siren's song on her lips. And when she stood near enough to touch him, she reached up and slowly unbuttoned her dress. The sheer fabric fell off her shoulders and puddled around her feet before the salt breeze caught it and blew the dress overboard. She laughed, the sound sweet and musical, lifted by the wind.

And then she fell into his arms, all warm skin and soft curves, and he kissed her. He knew he could never let her go, this woman, this wanton. His wife.

''THIS IS A WEDDING we're talking about, not a corporate takeover!''

Natalie Hillyard didn't respond at first, but continued down the sidewalk, dodging and weaving through the lunch hour pedestrians in downtown Boston. Her sister, Lydia, tried to keep up with her pace, but by the time they'd reached the lobby of the Donnelly Building, she was hopelessly out of breath, her face pink with the cold.

Natalie finally stopped and gave her sister a chance to recover. ''I don't see what you find so surprising. I have my entire wedding on a flow chart. I've timed every decision, every purchase and every event to the precise minute and dollar amount. And my flow chart says that you and I have to visit the florist after work at 5:37 p.m.'' She paused. ''Is that purple streak in your hair going to be gone by next month?''

Lydia reached up and touched her bangs. By the way they dressed, no one would ever guess they were sisters. Natalie was dressed in a tailored suit and cashmere overcoat. Save for the purple streak, Lydia was adorned in black befitting her image as an art student.

''Well, maybe your flow chart should have told you

to call me a few days ahead of time and let me know. I can't go, Natalie. I've got class.''

Natalie set her briefcase on a marble bench in the atrium lobby. ''I have all your classes on my scheduling software and you don't have a class tonight. You're my maid of honor, Lydie. The books say that you're supposed to help me with these things!''

''Nat, this is a wedding. The most important day of your life. You shouldn't have to do everything by the book.''

Frustrated, Natalie sat down on the bench, the tension of planning the wedding finally catching up with her. ''I'm sorry. It's just that this day has to be perfect. You don't know Edward's family. His mother would have been happy to plan and pay for the entire wedding herself, but it's important for me to prove my competency. Once I'm married to Edward, I'm going to have to organize our social events. I don't want her thinking I'm a complete nitwit.''

''And you want to marry into this family?'' Lydia ran her hands through her shaggy blond hair—hair the exact color of Natalie's, except for the purple streak. ''It's easy to be a blueblood if you've got a heart made of ice. That future mother-in-law of yours hasn't thawed in years.''

''Lydie, don't say that. They're going to be my family now. For the first time in my life, I'm going to have the security of a real family.''

A hurt expression crossed Lydia's face. ''*I'm* your family. Since Mom and Dad died, we've had each other, and that's always been enough. Nat, we've been through a lot in the last twenty years and we've survived. What do you need that stick Edward for? He doesn't deserve you."

"He's waited for me, through grad school, and then until I had my career established. He's a good man, Lydie, and I owe it to Edward to plan the most perfect wedding there ever was."

Lydia gasped. "Do you hear yourself? You *owe* it to Edward to marry him? You're supposed to marry Edward because you're madly in love with him and can't live without him. So far, I haven't once heard you say you love him. And you two spend more time apart than together."

Natalie bristled, Lydia's insight ringing truer than she wanted to admit. "You're twisting my words, because you don't like Edward. I happen to care for him...very deeply."

"See that? You can't even say the word!"

"Love? There, I said it! I love Edward."

Lydia crossed her arms over her chest and studied Natalie shrewdly. "I don't believe you."

"Well, I don't care. Besides, love is highly overrated. Edward and I respect each other. We share the same goals, the same outlook on life. Our marriage will be built on trust and companionship, not on lust."

Lydia groaned. "Oh, God, Nat. This is worse than I imagined. Tell me that you at least have a good sex life."

"My sex life is none of your business," Natalie said stubbornly. "And what's wrong with how I feel? Our parents supposedly loved each other, but they fought like cats and dogs right up until the very end.''

Lydia reached out and took Natalie's hand. ''I know that marrying Edward seems like a good idea, but I think you're marrying him for all the wrong reasons. Financial security and a houseful of interfering in-laws aren't good reasons.''

Natalie glanced at her watch, then slipped out of her coat and draped it over her arm. She picked up her briefcase and smoothed her skirt. ''I'm late. We're late. You were supposed to bring me back from lunch fifteen minutes early so that my staff could throw a bridal shower for me.''

''That was supposed to be a surprise,'' Lydia said, frowning.

''I *hate* surprises. Besides, I've had it on my flow chart for a week. I'm going to be late for the festivities. I'll see you tonight? Five thirty-seven at City Florists?''

Lydia nodded and Natalie kissed her sister on the cheek, then headed for the elevator, her thoughts occupied with Lydia's questions and doubts. Maybe she wasn't madly in love with Edward, but they would base their marriage on something much less fickle than emotion. She had always been a practical person, someone who preferred fact to fantasy, good sense to sentiment. And she'd been lucky enough to find a man who shared her pragmatic outlook on life.

Most people might call Edward stuffy and maybe even a little boring. But in him, Natalie found all the stability and security she'd lost the day her parents had died. From that instant on, her life had been filled with endless upheaval as she and her little sister were shuffled from relative to foster home and back again. Edward would always provide a good home for her and that's all she really needed to be happy.

Glancing at her watch again, she pushed the button on the elevator, then tapped her foot impatiently. She really was behind schedule. Hopefully, the ladies in the office would present her with one large gift rather than lots of little gifts to be unwrapped, a waste of precious time. Why they'd insisted on throwing a wedding shower, she wasn't sure. They were her staff, not her friends. The work setting was no place to make friends.

The elevator finally arrived and Natalie swept inside. The doors were just about to close behind her when she heard a male voice call out, "Hold the elevator!" When an arm snaked between the doors setting off the sensor, she reached out and pushed the button to close them. She didn't have time to wait for stragglers. He could catch the next elevator.

The door began to shut, but the man stuck his hand in again. Back and forth they went, the doors closing and opening and closing and opening until the stranger finally cursed out loud and shoved his shoulder between them. Natalie snatched her hand from the control panel and moved back, pasting a polite smile on her face.

He stepped into the doorway, annoyance flooding his handsome features. But then he stopped short and stared at her, unblinking and unabashed. He opened his mouth to speak, but then snapped it shut, frowning. Still he watched her, and she couldn't help but look back. After all, he was incredibly handsome, with chiseled features like she'd only seen in fashion ads.

A bizarre current of attraction crackled between them and a shiver skittered up her spine, but still she couldn't look away. He had the most beautiful green eyes that she'd ever seen—clear and direct, without a trace of artifice. Throughout her childhood, to protect herself and her sister, she had been forced to evaluate strangers in such a way, to read the motives behind their eyes. There was nothing to fear from this man, of that she was certain.

Then why did she suddenly feel so breathless? Sure, he was handsome. Any woman would find him attractive. But it was the way that he looked at her, as if he were slowly undressing her with his eyes. Never in her life had a man looked at her like that—not even Edward. Nor did she expect him to, for Natalie knew she wasn't particularly pretty.

She forced herself to glance away, to fix her eyes on the control panel to her right. But she was drawn inexplicably back to him, sneaking another peek when the doors began to close. For an instant, she wondered if she should get out. But she was already seven minutes late, and Natalie hated to be late. She also hated people who ignored the unspoken rules of elevator etiquette. This handsome stranger didn't face the door and turn his attention to the lights above it. Instead, he continued to stare at her, almost as if he recognized her.

Natalie took a small step sideways, wondering if maybe they did know each other. But she would have remembered this man—those perfect features, the deep tan that hinted of a winter spent in southern climes. His dark hair, blown by the wind, was longer than proper business style dictated, brushing the collar of his leather jacket.

Her gaze slid over his long, lean body before she turned her eyes up to the lights above the door. Instead of a suit, he wore jeans and a khaki-colored shirt and—her gaze ground to a halt—a tie with a hand-painted hula dancer. She stifled a smile and looked down at her shoes.

"Do we know each other?" His voice, rich and warm, echoed through the elevator car.

For a moment, she wondered if he was talking to her. But then she realized that he had to be—they were the only two people in the elevator. Her heart skipped, not out of fear, but out of some strange excitement. She turned to speak, then looked away.

All her common sense told her to ignore this man, but she couldn't. Except for the tie, he didn't seem like the type to test his favorite pickup lines on strange women in elevators. But why would he turn his attention on her? "No," she finally murmured. "I don't believe we do."

"Funny. I could have sworn..."

She glanced over at him and found herself smiling. "I have a very good memory for names and faces. And I'm sure we've never met."

They continued the elevator ride in silence and had

nearly reached her floor when the stranger leaned in front of her and flipped a switch on the control panel. The elevator bumped to a halt.

"This is going to sound strange," he said, "but I think I know where we've met."

She should have been frightened now, caught in an elevator that was going nowhere, a strange man her only companion. But she wasn't. For all the common sense that Natalie possessed, she knew this man didn't mean her any harm. In fact, she felt flattered by his attention. "I'm sure we haven't..."

He raked his fingers through his hair, then held out his hand. "All right. It was in my dream last night." He paused. "You. You were in my dream. We were on a sailboat and I was...well, that doesn't really matter."

Natalie smiled again. This was certainly the most original line she'd ever heard, though she would have expected something smoother, more sophisticated. But she did take some small pleasure in the fact that, for the very first time, a man was trying a line on her. "This is all very amusing, but I'm engaged."

Her statement seemed to take him by complete surprise and he frowned. "But you can't be," he said. "You're supposed to marry me."

Natalie's eyes went wide and suddenly her common sense returned in full force. This man was not just handsome. He was crazy, whacko, a certified lunatic. She quickly reached over and flipped the switch he'd touched. The elevator began to move again, but only until the stranger flipped the switch again.

Natalie's anger rose. Who was this guy? And what right did he have to hold her hostage in an elevator? "Listen, mister, I don't know what you want, but if you don't—"

"Wait! Just hear me out. I swear, I'm not crazy."

"I don't want to listen to you," she cried. "I'm late and I'm engaged. And nothing you say to me is going to make a difference."

He closed his eyes and shook his head. "You're right." He reached across her and started the elevator once again. "It's just that my grandmother had this vision. And she's never wrong. And then you were there, in my dream. And now you're here. And somewhere between the birthday cake and this elevator, I've completely lost my mind." He cursed softly, then gave her a sideways glance. "You wouldn't want to have dinner with me tonight, would you?"

Natalie couldn't help but laugh. The sound bubbling from her throat surprised her, for she rarely found much that genuinely amused her. But this handsome stranger had an uncanny way of undermining her customary self-restraint. "I told you, I'm engaged."

"And I'm Chase," he said, holding out his hand. "Short for Charles. It's nice to meet you. Maybe we could meet for coffee after work?"

Hesitantly, she clutched her hands together in front of her, certain that the moment she touched him her resolve would disappear and she'd fall victim to his considerable charms. "I—I don't care what your name is. And I don't drink coffee. I'm engaged."

"Tea, then? I know—you're engaged. But if you

don't drink something, you're going to get dehydrated.''

She shook her head, tempted to say yes, but determined that she would not allow herself to consider his offer. She looked up at the numbers above the door. Why was this elevator moving so slowly? And why was this man, this Chase, this *stranger* having such a disconcerting effect on her?

Natalie Hillyard did not speak to strangers! Not on the street, not in the subway and not on an elevator. Not even if the stranger was the most handsome man she'd ever met. She didn't accept impromptu invitations and she certainly didn't fall for tired old pickup lines.

''Water,'' he said. ''We could go out and have a nice glass of water.''

''No!'' she replied. To her relief, the elevator doors finally opened on her floor. She hurried out, glancing over her shoulder to make sure he wasn't following her. But he just stood, his shoulder braced against the open door, and gave her a wave. ''You'd like me,'' he said. ''People say I'm a really nice guy.''

''And I'm engaged!''

Chase laughed, the warm sound filling the hallway. She reached for the door to the reception area and pulled it open, determined to put as much distance between her and this sexy stranger as she could.

''We will meet again, sweetheart,'' he called as the door slowly swung closed behind her. ''It's destiny.''

Chapter Two

"IT'S ABOUT TIME you got here! You were supposed to come this morning."

Chase shoved his hands in his jacket pockets. He hadn't expected a warm welcome. "Nice to see you too, baby brother. Sorry I'm late. The elevator was... temporarily stuck."

"Our elevators are always in perfect working order," John said, his bluster an exact imitation of Chase's father. "I'm going to have to speak with maintenance about this."

Chase waved him off. "Leave it for later. It's not important."

"Never leave for tomorrow what can be done today," John replied.

"Wait, let me write that down," Chase said. "I want to embroider it on a pillow."

John sighed in exasperation. "I can see that this is going to be a waste of time. I don't know why you bothered to show up."

Chase clapped his brother on the shoulder. "Don't despair, Johnny. Now that I'm here, I'd love to take a tour of the office. You can introduce me to all the little people."

Actually, there was only one person Chase was interested in meeting. Somewhere in the office he'd find his dream girl, the pretty blonde who had left him standing at the elevator door just moments ago.

When he had first stepped inside the elevator and caught sight of her face, he'd felt as if someone had punched him hard in the gut. His breath froze and his vision blurred, and for a moment, he had tried to convince himself that she didn't look familiar at all, that she was merely an attractive stranger.

But his dream the night before had been so vivid, leaving every detail of her face and her body imprinted on his mind. She was the one—the one his grandmother had told him about. She was no longer a dream, but a real flesh-and-blood woman. And if Nana's prediction was to be believed, she would someday be Chase's wife.

Though he'd learned to believe in Nana Tonya's visions, he still couldn't help but search for a logical explanation for the woman's appearance. Had he met her before? Did she merely resemble the woman in his dreams? Or was she, as his grandmother claimed, part of his destiny?

He didn't have answers for the jumble of questions that followed, but he knew he had to see her again. She'd been bound for the corporate offices of Donnelly Enterprises. If he was lucky, she was an employee with a desk and a nameplate. And if she wasn't, the receptionist would certainly remember her arrival—and her name.

"I suppose we could start with a tour of the offices," John grumbled. "I could introduce you to our management team, although many of them will still be at lunch. If you've been reading our corporate newsletter, you know that we've consolidated several divisions under—"

"Can the commentary, brother. Just give me the tour. I'll ask any questions as they come up."

The tour seemed to drag on for hours, although Chase knew it wasn't taking nearly as much time. He found corporate life exceedingly dull. Marketing, operations, data processing, personnel; endless offices and endless introductions...

As they entered the finance department, Chase was ready to give up and trust that the receptionist could provide him with more illuminating information. He turned to John, but then a group of women crowded into a small, glass-walled conference room caught his eye. He stopped short as one of the women held up a lacy black negligee.

"She's the one," Chase murmured, stopping to stare through the window.

"What?"

"Who is that?" he asked. "There. With the lacy underwear."

John shook his head in disgust and clucked his tongue. "I wouldn't have expected such unprofessional behavior from Natalie Hillyard. But I guess all women lose a little of their common sense before their wedding. She's getting married next month, but thank God, she's not taking a honeymoon. Ms. Hillyard is our director of finance. Runs the whole department. In a few more years she'll be in line for a vice presidency—that is, unless she decides to dump her career for kids and a house in the suburbs.''

''She's beautiful.''

John frowned as he stared through the window. ''Beautiful? Natalie Hillyard?''

Chase nodded. Though most men would probably miss it, Natalie Hillyard had a simple perfection about her, an inner radiance that seemed to illuminate features that many men might find unremarkable—pale hair and high cheekbones, wide green eyes and delicate mouth. But Chase saw much more. A vulnerability that she managed to hide behind a dispassionate expression.

''Don't even think about it, Chase. She's engaged and she's a very competent, valued employee. M.B.A. from Boston College. Comes to work at seven every morning and doesn't leave until seven at night. Definitely not your type.''

''Her name is Natalie Hillyard?''

''Donnellys do not pursue employees of the company. If you even approach her, I'm going to tell Father.''

''You always were a tattletale, Johnny.'' Chase sighed. ''Come on, you can introduce me.''

Chase stepped through the door of the conference room, taking in the balloons and crepe paper decorations, the cake displayed on a long credenza. The festive chatter stopped the moment the ladies noticed his presence, but Chase's attention was firmly focused on Natalie Hillyard. He grinned, then nodded at the lacy confection she held in her hand. "Very nice," he said. "The latest in business attire, I presume."

The flush of color that had accompanied her perusal of the gift drained from her face and Natalie Hillyard blinked in surprise. "It's you," she murmured, white-knuckled fingers clutching the lacy lingerie.

John cleared his throat and stepped in front of Chase. "Ladies, I'd like to introduce my older brother, Charles Donnelly IV. Chase, these women work in our financial department."

Chase slowly circled the room, shaking hands with each one and enjoying a personal introduction. Low whispers followed him and he knew they were speculating about his sudden appearance. According to his father, Chase was the subject of endless gossip, though he rarely set foot in the office.

When he reached Natalie Hillyard, he again held out his hand. "Miss Hillyard. Best wishes on your upcoming wedding." He glanced down at the open boxes of lingerie, then fingered a pale green teddy. "The green suits you," he said, leaning closer so that only she could hear his words.

Color came back to her cheeks and her hand grew limp in his. "It—it's a pleasure to meet you, Mr. Donnelly."

"Chase," he said. "After all, we're old friends, aren't we?"

She murmured his name once before fumbling with the open boxes of lingerie. Chase watched her for a long moment, then turned back to John. "Nana tells me that I have an office here. Why don't you show me where it is? I can count my paper clips while you get back to work.''

John sighed in exasperation, then turned and headed out the door. Chase took one last look at Natalie Hillyard, then smiled to himself. To hell with corporate policy. A guy didn't dream of the girl he was supposed to marry, then just walk away from her without another word.

''Ladies, it was my pleasure.''

The group burst into a clamor of conversation the moment he stepped out of the room. He didn't even bother to speculate as to the subject. If Natalie Hillyard hadn't heard of his reputation by now, she certainly would by the end of the day. Chase winced inwardly. For once he wished that his reputation hadn't preceded him.

They reached an office three doors past John's and entered. The interior looked much like his brother's office without the requisite family photos and college rowing trophies. Chase circled his desk, then flopped down into his chair and propped his feet up on the smooth mahogany surface. He wove his fingers together behind his head. ''Nice,'' he murmured. ''Do I have a secretary?''

John, being devoid of a sense of humor, found nothing funny about Chase's question. He crossed his arms over his chest and sent his brother a warning glare. ''Don't bother the employees and don't make any long distance calls on business phones. If you have any questions, I'm 8674 on the intercom.''

Chase swiveled around in his chair. ''Does the computer work?''

''You can access anything that's not confidential—even executive-level information. There's a list of commands in your top desk drawer. Use the last six digits of your social security number as your password.''

Chase waited until his brother closed the door before he spun around in his chair and flipped on his computer. He grabbed the command list from the desk drawer and set to work. ''Natalie Hillyard,'' he murmured. ''Let's get to know each other a little better.''

A few minutes later, he had a personnel profile, a résumé of sorts that gave her educational background and history with the company. Her address and home phone was easy enough to get from the company directory. He scribbled it on a piece of scrap paper and shoved it in his pocket.

But then he bumbled into something completely unexpected, better than her home phone number. The computer system at Donnelly Enterprises included a scheduling program for employees to keep track of their business appointments. Sweet Natalie also kept her personal schedule on the computer.

''City Florists,'' Chase read. ''Five thirty-seven. Tonight.'' With a satisfied smile, he hit the print command and waited for the rest of Natalie's schedule to appear.

As he watched the paper slip from the printer, he wondered at his sudden obsession with this woman. It wasn't as if he was certain they were meant for each other. But he was curious. Would she turn out to be the same extraordinary woman he'd made love to in his dreams? Or would fantasy prove to be much more alluring than reality?

Chase had had his share of fantasy females—beautiful, sexy women who drifted in and out of his life as regularly as the tide. Not one of them had captured his attention as Natalie had. She was a mystery, a cool facade impenetrable at first contact. Yet there was so much more hidden beneath the surface. Why did the thought of exploring her depths fascinate him so?

Whenever he'd imagined himself married and raising a family, he'd always pictured a woman like Natalie by his side—tall and slender, fresh faced, confident and intelligent. A woman he could spend a lifetime getting to know, someone more complex than just a pretty face and a sexy body.

Chase leaned back in his chair and stared at the ceiling. What the hell was he doing? He'd shared no more than a few minutes with Natalie Hillyard and already he was picturing her as a permanent fixture in his life. Had he completely lost his mind?

She was engaged, a point she'd made patently clear more than once. Pursuing her would probably turn out to be a total waste of time. Still, there had to be something to Nana's vision. He'd dreamed of a woman and that woman had appeared before him the very next day, in the flesh. A man couldn't ignore such a singular event. Chase had always been one to test his own destiny and now was no exception. He needed to prove that Natalie Hillyard was not the woman of his dreams—or he'd have to marry her.

Chase flipped off his computer and grabbed the copy of Natalie's schedule. He methodically folded it in thirds, then shoved it in the back pocket of his jeans as he reviewed his options.

Natalie was an employee of Donnelly Enterprises and, according to John, took her job very seriously. No doubt she'd be reluctant to date a Donnelly, but since Chase didn't work for the company, that problem could probably be overcome. Beyond that, he'd simply need to deal with her insistence that she was happily engaged and about to be married.

What had John said? She'd be married next month? Chase snatched the schedule from his pocket and flipped through the pages. "April 4." He cursed softly to himself. That was only two weeks away. Two weeks to determine if Natalie Hillyard really was his destiny. And if she was, what then? Somehow he sensed that life would be a lot easier if he just forgot about his dream girl and walked away.

But Chase Donnelly had spent his life making every dream he had ever had come true. He wasn't about to toss this one aside.

A COLD SPRING RAIN dampened rush hour as Natalie approached City Florists at precisely 5:36 p.m., one minute before she'd told Lydia to arrive. Their appointment wasn't until quarter to six, but on average, Lydia arrived for most events approximately eight minutes late. It was always best to take her sister's tardy habits into account.

Natalie's first visit to the florist had been exactly three months prior to her wedding date, but she had insisted on approving a sample of the centerpieces to be certain the lilies fit in exactly with her color scheme. Mother Jennings would not tolerate tiny imperfections.

Given the choice, Natalie would have been happy with a small civil service. Without family of her own, the wedding was no more than a party for Edward, his parents and their numerous friends, relatives and business associates. But one did not become a Jennings without a very proper and very formal ceremony and reception.

Natalie pulled open the door, then wrestled her umbrella inside. As she turned, she caught sight of the only other customer in the shop. He stood with his back to her, speaking to the clerk behind the counter. There was something so familiar about him—the dark hair brushing his collar, the leather jacket, the blue jeans that hugged his—

She froze. What was *he* doing here? Cursing softly, she scurried behind a huge palm, peering through the fronds at the man who had bedeviled her thoughts for the entire afternoon. Chase Donnelly turned to look at a bucket of daffodils, and Natalie stared, transfixed by his handsome profile.

Time after time she'd caught herself thinking about their encounter in the elevator, about the odd attraction she'd felt toward him, the jolt of electricity that had tingled through her body when he'd taken her hand. She couldn't recall ever experiencing such an immediate and disturbing sensation. Even when she'd first met Edward there had been only a mild interest. But this man—Chase Donnelly—was different than any man she'd ever met.

"He's dangerous," she murmured to herself.

"Who's dangerous?"

Startled, Natalie turned to find Lydia standing at her shoulder and staring toward Chase. She grabbed Lydia by the arm and yanked her behind the potted palm. Lydia gave a little yelp and Natalie clapped her hand over his sister's mouth. "What are you doing here?" she whispered.

"You asked me to come," Lydia said, tugging at Natalie's fingers.

"You're early."

Lydia slapped at Natalie's hand. "What are you doing? And why are we whispering?"

"He's here," Natalie said in a miserable voice. She sneaked another peek through the fronds. "Over there. Looking at the daffodils."

"Who?"

"Chase Donnelly. I—I met him in the elevator. I mean, I didn't really meet him. We—"

"Donnelly as in Donnelly Enterprises?" A frown marred Lydia's forehead. "Why are you hiding from him?"

"I'm not hiding."

"Is he your boss?"

"Technically, he doesn't work for the company. But

he's on the board of directors, so he could have me fired if he wanted to. And after the elevator, and then the wedding shower, well, I—''

''What elevator? Nat, you're babbling and you never babble.''

''Do you think he followed me?'' Natalie shook her head ''No. He couldn't have. He was here when I got here. He didn't follow me. It's just...a coincidence.'' She paused and sighed. ''Fate,'' she murmured. ''Destiny,'' she added, recalling his words to her.

''Then why are you hiding in the bushes? He probably won't even recognize you.''

''Oh, he'll remember me,'' Natalie said, glancing at Lydia. ''He says I'm supposed to marry him. He dreamed it in a dream. Something about his grandmother and birthday cake. I didn't quite understand. It was all a little...overwhelming.''

Lydia's eyes grew wide and she turned to stare at Natalie. ''You're kidding. Your boss told you that you were going to marry him? Is he crazy?''

''Probably. And he's not my boss. He's just related to my boss,'' Natalie repeated. ''Maybe that's why he never comes into the office. Maybe the family keeps him hidden away because he has...mental problems.'' She drew a long breath. ''Could a guy that handsome really be a lunatic? He has the kindest eyes. And a little dimple in his chin and...'' Lydia stepped out from behind the plants, but Natalie pulled her back. ''Where are you going?''

''I'm going to check him out.''

"If you talk to him, tell him to leave me alone. Tell him I'm engaged."

Natalie watched as her sister casually strolled over to the counter. Lydia had always been much more assertive than Natalie, more willing to take chances. And she'd always been more comfortable around strangers—especially men.

At first, Lydia stood at a safe distance, studying Chase surreptitiously while she spun a rack of greeting cards. But then, to Natalie's consternation, her sister struck up a conversation with him. Before long, they were chatting amiably. A thread of what felt like jealousy snaked through her and she turned away, scolding herself silently.

What was wrong with her? All these strange feelings welling up inside of her did nothing but frighten and confuse her. She was never one to act on impulse, to behave irrationally. But this man brought out the worst in her character, flaws she'd never known about.

"Natalie?"

She spun back around. To her mortification, Lydia was crossing the shop with Chase in tow. Frantically, Natalie glanced toward the door, calculating the odds on making a clean getaway. But she couldn't run. She needed to put an end to this ridiculous situation as soon as possible.

"Natalie, look who I just met!" Lydia cried. "It's Chase Donnelly. Chase, you know my sister, Natalie Hillyard."

With a smile quirking the corners of his mouth, he held out his hand, daring her once again to place her fingers in his. She found herself transfixed by his handsome face, her gaze skimming over the strong planes and angles, lingering on his vivid green eyes and the cleft in his chin. Her mind swam, a whirlpool of confusion and attraction and frustration. Their gazes locked.

"It's nice to see you again, Natalie," he said, a teasing tone in his voice.

His fingers were warm and strong, and a familiar tingle seeped up her arm, numbing her nerves like a potent drug. She felt a slow blush creep up her cheeks as she struggled to find her voice. When she tried to draw her hand away, he held tight to her fingers. "What—what are you doing here...Mr. Donnelly?"

"I just stopped in to order some flowers," he replied. "For my grandmother."

"Did you hear that, Natalie?" Lydia said, her voice sounding a million miles away. "He's buying flowers for his grandmother. Isn't that nice?" She lowered her voice and bent near. "Not the actions of a crazy man, I think."

"Yes," Natalie breathed. "Very nice."

Chase slowly rubbed his thumb along the back of her hand and Natalie lost herself in the enjoyment of the simple caress. "I'm really glad we had another chance to meet. It gives me an opportunity to apologize for my behavior this morning in the elevator. I'm sure I must have sounded like a real kook."

"Yes," Natalie replied, staring down at her hand. "I—I mean, no. Not at all."

"Would it be too forward to ask if you'd care to

join me for coffee after you're finished here?'' he asked. ''I'd like to make it up to you.''

''Yes,'' she murmured, willing to say anything to stop the barrage of sensations that raced through her body. ''I mean, it wouldn't be too forward to ask.''

''Good. I'll meet you then. At Jitterbug's. It's right down the block. In a half hour?''

''Jitterbug's,'' Natalie replied absently. ''Yes, it's right down the block.''

With that, he let go of her hand and started toward the door. He turned back once and smiled at her, then walked out of the shop. She wasn't sure how long she stood there, staring at the door and rubbing the back of her hand. Had it not been for Lydia, she probably would have stood there all night.

''Oh my,'' Lydia said with a sigh. ''Did you just accept a date with him?''

Natalie blinked. ''No, of course not,'' she replied, her mind frantically racing through their conversation. ''I didn't, did I? I told him it wasn't forward of him to ask. But I didn't accept.''

''I think you did.''

Natalie grabbed her sister's elbow and clutched it tightly. ''I can't meet him for coffee. I'm engaged.''

''Don't yell at me! You're the one who accepted the invitation.''

''Why didn't you stop me?'' Natalie demanded. She pulled Lydia toward the counter at the back of the store. ''Have you forgotten why we're here? We're here to discuss the flowers for my wedding.''

"What wedding? I think you should forget Edward. I like this guy much better."

"Forget Edward? How can I forget my fiancé?"

"Where is he, anyway?" Lydia asked. "Shouldn't he be here, helping you with the wedding? He's never around when he's supposed to be."

"Edward is in London on business, where he will be for the next week."

"Good. Then you can meet Chase for coffee after we're finished here and no one will be the wiser."

"Lydia, why are you doing this? If rumor is to be believed, Chase Donnelly is a certified Casanova."

"Because I think you deserve better than Edward Jennings and that pack of vultures he calls a family." She sighed longingly. "And this guy is *definitely* better, don't you think?"

Natalie glanced back at the door, then cursed this sudden impulsiveness that had come over her. What was she doing? Her whole life had been planned out, beginning with a fairy-tale wedding to a man she'd known for years. And now, out of the blue, she had accepted a date with a complete stranger—and a reputed playboy to boot.

"Prewedding nerves," she murmured. "All brides go through their moments of doubt, don't they?"

"Sure," Lydia said, "although most of them just have a good cry and then feel better. But a date for coffee with a handsome man—that's another approach."

The truth was, Natalie wanted to go. She wanted to find out why Chase Donnelly had such a hold on her, why her attraction to him seemed to overwhelm every bit of her common sense and decency. And she wanted, once and for all, to put an end to all the silly feelings he stirred up inside of her.

She moaned and pressed her fingers into her temples. "I won't go. I can't go. After all, I'm engaged."

HE WAS SITTING at a table by the window when she arrived. His hair was damp from the rain and he had slicked it back from his face with his fingers. His profile was even more handsome, his tan skin gleaming in the bright lights of the café.

Drawing on her resolve, Natalie strode over to his table. She held her breath as he looked up at her, but she deliberately avoided his eyes. "This is a mistake," she said, her voice firm and even. "I didn't mean to accept your invitation. I misunderstood."

He leaned back in his chair and crossed his arms over his chest, sending her a dubious look. "But you're here now," he noted. "If you didn't want to come, why didn't you just stand me up?"

Natalie shifted, asking herself the same question and unable to come up with an answer. "I—I..." She swallowed hard. "That wouldn't be polite. After all, I do technically work for you. It's best to cultivate a proper professional relationship, don't you think?"

He considered her reply for a long moment, the silence growing between them until she was forced to look into his eyes. "Come on, Natalie," he said with a charming grin. "Admit it. You're as curious as I am."

She tipped her chin up. ''About what?''

''About this thing that's going on between us.''

Natalie stiffened and tried to maintain her composure. ''There's nothing between us. You're a complete stranger to me. I don't even know you. How can there be anything between us?''

''We're attracted to each other,'' Chase said, so bluntly that he made it sound like fact. ''I felt it the minute I walked into the elevator. You're just too stubborn to admit it.''

Natalie closed her eyes and shook her head. ''No... no, I'm not.''

He picked up his coffee cup and took a sip. ''You're not stubborn or you're not attracted to me?''

''Attracted,'' she said.

''Then I'll ask you again. Why are you here?''

Natalie had had enough of this cat and mouse game he insisted on playing. ''All right!'' she said, her jaw tight with annoyance. ''Maybe I am attracted to you. But that doesn't mean I'm going to act on my feelings. I want you to forget about our encounter in the elevator. And I'm going to forget about accepting your invitation for coffee. We'll just pretend like none of this ever happened.''

Chase shook his head. ''I can't do that, Natalie. I won't. Not until I know for sure.''

''I have to leave,'' Natalie said, confused by his cryptic words.

As she turned, Chase shoved his chair back and grabbed her hand. She tried to pull away, but he held tight. Gently, he twisted her around until she faced him. He hooked his finger under her chin and forced her to meet his eyes.

For a moment, she was certain he was going to kiss her. Her gaze slipped down to his mouth, to sculpted lips that were parted slightly. If this simple touch had such a profound effect on her, how would she ever be able to resist his mouth and his tongue, the feel of his hands on her body?

"I don't want you to kiss me," she murmured.

A smile touched the corners of his mouth. "I wasn't planning to. Not yet."

Natalie glanced up to see humor sparkling in his eyes, and she felt a warm flush of embarrassment heat her cheeks.

"Just stay, for a little while," he said. He pulled out her chair. "Sit. We can talk."

Worn down by the power of his charming smile, she reluctantly did as he asked. He motioned a waitress over to their table and Natalie placed an order for a café *latte.* She wrapped her arms around herself and waited for him to speak.

"Why don't you take off your coat?"

"I'm not planning to stay long."

The waitress reappeared with Natalie's coffee, thankfully providing a distraction from the silence that had settled at their table. The hot brew burned her throat as she hurried to drink it. The sooner she finished, the sooner she could leave.

"When I stepped inside that elevator, you took me by surprise."

Natalie looked over at him, only to find Chase studying her intently.

''It was like we'd already met. Do you believe in fate, Natalie?''

She would have liked to believe in fate. It would have explained her parents' death and all the things in her childhood that had followed. But Natalie could only believe in cold, hard facts. The skid marks from her parents' car. The truck driver who had fallen asleep behind the wheel. The police knocking at the front door late at night. And the awful feeling of desertion she and Lydia had had. She'd been thirteen when it had happened, all alone in the world except for her six-year-old sister.

Natalie shook her head, brushing aside the bitter memories. ''No, I don't. Everything happens for a reason and you just have to look closely to find a logical explanation.''

''And our meeting?''

''I was returning from lunch—I was late. And you were...what were you doing in the office?''

''An attempt at family harmony,'' he said.

''So it wasn't fate. We were both supposed to be right where we were.''

''And now we're here. Having coffee together. So, Natalie, why don't you tell me about yourself?''

''I'm engaged,'' she repeated, for what seemed like the millionth time.

''And what would your fiancé have to say if he knew you were having coffee with me?''

Natalie opened her mouth to reply, then snapped it

shut. To be honest, Edward probably wouldn't say a word. He wasn't prone to jealousy, not that she'd ever given him a reason to be jealous. Edward never displayed an excessive level of emotion. He was a very... controlled man. "We trust each other completely," she finally answered.

Chase chuckled. "If you were my fiancée, I wouldn't be so magnanimous."

Natalie had always wondered what it would be like to have a man feel so passionately about her, to care for her so much that he'd be jealous. But then, Chase's remark shouldn't surprise her. He seemed to be driven purely by impulse, by emotions that she couldn't even begin to fathom.

"But you aren't my fiancé," Natalie said. "You aren't even my friend. I've heard all about you, Chase Donnelly, and don't think I can't see right through your charm."

"Then tell me the truth, Natalie. Are you really happy with this fiancé of yours?"

Her head snapped up and she met his gaze. "Edward is everything I've ever wanted in a husband," she said, trying to keep her voice sure and even. "And nothing anyone says is going to stop me from marrying him."

Chase stared at her for a long moment, then pushed back from the table and stood. "All right. Fine." He reached into his pocket and withdrew his wallet, then tossed a few bills on the table. "Hell, I thought I'd give it a shot. A guy can't ignore destiny, can he?"

Natalie shook her head. "No, I guess not."

Chase smiled ruefully, then bent down and brushed a kiss on her cheek. "It's been wonderful not falling in love with you, Natalie Hillyard. Take care of yourself."

With that, he turned and walked out the door into the drizzling night. She watched him through the window, craning her neck as the other pedestrians gradually hid him from view.

She took a deep breath and slowly arranged the items on the table—first her coffee cup and saucer, then her napkin and spoon—putting everything in perfect order. When she'd finished, she placed her palms on the table and gathered her thoughts.

"I've just had a very bad day," she murmured to herself. "Tomorrow, everything will be back to normal. My life will be right on track."

She sat in the coffee shop for a long time, staring out the window and trying to convince herself of the truth of her words. But somehow, she knew that nothing would ever be the same again. She knew that she would always wonder where this day might have led, had she been willing to throw caution to the wind and take a chance.

Chapter Three

THE DELIVERIES BEGAN arriving the next morning, just as Natalie was finally getting to sleep. She had passed a restless night, tossing and turning, plagued by fitful dreams—of a dark-haired man with a roguish smile juxtaposed with her wedding, a day filled with mistakes and mishaps and a driving rainstorm.

Exhausted, she had rolled out of bed in the middle of the night and sat down with all her wedding files, alphabetizing her response cards, adjusting her budget and pouring over the seating charts that her future mother-in-law had provided. But the more she thought about her impending nuptials, the more restless Natalie grew.

She had tried in vain to call Edward in London, hoping that a quick conversation with him would put all to rights. But after numerous attempts to reach him, she had finally dozed off on the sofa, the shopping channel blaring away on cable. Not long after the sun had risen, she was awakened by the doorbell.

Dragging herself to the door, Natalie pulled her robe around her and brushed her hair out of her eyes. She expected the paperboy or someone collecting for charity, but instead she found a huge bouquet of yellow daffodils awaiting her.

Natalie didn't need to look at the card to guess who

they were from. Edward had never in his life sent her flowers, and she was certain he had no reason to start now. The daffodils could be from only one person—Chase Donnelly.

Perturbed, she gathered the bouquet in her arms and wandered back to the kitchen to find a vase. Fifteen minutes later, the next delivery arrived, followed by another every quarter hour. But there were no more flowers. Just a strange assortment of items—fresh baked baguettes and cheese, a tin of oysters, three different bottles of wine, a box of expensive Belgian chocolates, a basket of fresh fruit.

With every delivery, Natalie scanned the street, checking to make sure her nosy neighbors in Redmond were tucked safely inside their houses. Living in the same small town as Edward's parents caused Natalie no end of stress. But Edward had insisted on buying the huge house on Birch Street, determined to fashion a life in the exact image of his very proper parents.

Of course, it would have been highly *im*proper for Edward to share a residence with Natalie before they married, so he had left her alone there in the huge, cavernous house, empty of furniture and badly in need of refurbishing. Once they were married, they would work on the house together, he promised. And though Natalie would have been quite happy with a tiny little cottage in the country, life with Edward meant living in a hundred-year-old mansion that seemed perpetually empty.

By eleven, Natalie's foyer looked like an explosion in a delicatessen. For some strange reason, Chase was under the impression that the way to a woman's heart was through her stomach, and he intended to see her very well fed. Had she known his phone number, she would have called to demand that he cease and desist.

When the doorbell rang again, Natalie had just stepped out of the shower. Cursing Chase Donnelly and his gifts, she hurried to the door and flung it open, ready to give the delivery man an earful. But it was Chase, leaning against the doorjamb, a devilish grin on his lips. ''Good morning,'' he said. ''You look pretty with your hair all wet.'' He bent closer and stole a quick kiss, the same way he'd done the night before. So casually, as if he'd kissed her a hundred times in the past.

Clutching her robe at her throat, Natalie scanned the street, then dragged him inside, slamming the door behind him. ''What are you doing here? How did you find me?''

He glanced around the huge foyer, his gaze taking in all the gifts scattered about the floor. ''Is that any way to greet a friend?''

''You're not my friend,'' Natalie said, stamping her bare foot on the cold marble floor.

''Then is that any way to greet an acquaintance you barely tolerate?''

''How did you find me?''

Chase shrugged. ''I could say I hired a private detective. Or that I followed you home last night. But to tell the truth, I hacked into the employee files at the office.'' She watched as he wandered toward the wide central staircase, peering into each room along the way. "You actually live here? This place is huge."

"Edward and I bought it a month after we set our wedding date. You have to leave. If anyone saw you come in I'll—"

"So, does he live here, too? I'd really like to meet him. Is he home?"

Natalie shook her head. "He's out of town on business. He'll move in after the wedding. Right now, he lives with his parents."

"Too bad," Chase murmured. "It always pays to know the competition." He slowly turned and raised his eyebrow. "You know, it would take an army to keep me out of my bride's bed before the wedding. He must be a very disciplined man."

Natalie sighed in frustration, certain that Chase's comment was meant more as an insult than a compliment. "Why are you here? I thought I made it clear last night that I didn't want anything to do with you."

"You did. But I didn't believe you. Let's just say you were less than convincing. Especially when we were holding hands in the flower shop. Remember that?"

"Vaguely."

"You wanted me to kiss you. I could see it in your eyes."

"I—I wanted nothing of the sort."

He stepped closer until they were nearly touching. She could feel the heat of his body, the soft caress of his warm breath at her temple. Natalie wanted to step away, but she couldn't bring herself to move. All her resolve slowly melted beneath his intense gaze.

She wasn't prepared for what happened next, yet it seemed the most natural thing in the world. He kissed her, long and deep, his mouth consuming hers in a flood of pure desire. Natalie's knees went weak and he grabbed her around the waist and pulled her up against his lean, hard body. Her mind spun in confusion, but no matter how hard she tried, she couldn't summon the power to push him away.

Passion like she'd never experienced before raced through her blood, setting her nerves on fire, testing all her notions of self-control. Her every thought now centered on his mouth, on the taste of his tongue, the play of his lips across hers. She felt instantly alive and aware. She felt wanted and needed, beyond all common sense and propriety.

Natalie had kissed only one man in her entire life with any degree of passion, and that had been Edward. But nothing she had ever experienced with Edward came close to the power of Chase's mouth on hers. Like an addictive drug, his kiss numbed her brain until she could do nothing more than succumb to the wonderful surge of pure sensation.

But then a brief instant of clarity returned as she realized the magnitude of her actions. With a tiny cry, she pulled out of his arms and brought her fingers to her swollen lips. "I—I've cheated," she said, misery flooding her voice. "I'm engaged and I've just cheated on my fiancé."

Chase stared down at her for a long moment, the

passion that glazed his eyes slowly clearing. Then he bit back a curse. "I—I'm sorry, Natalie. I shouldn't have done that. It wasn't fair."

"No, no. It's my fault," Natalie said, turning to pace the length of the foyer. "I wanted you to kiss me." She stopped and pressed her fingers against her temples. "I don't know what's happening to me. I'm supposed to be engaged and I'm kissing a perfect stranger."

Chase grabbed her by the arms and forced her gaze up to his. "If you really felt something, Natalie, and you ignore it, the only person you're cheating is yourself."

"I have no choice. What just happened was a mistake. An error in judgment. We'll just...put it behind us. Like it never happened."

"But it did happen. And I'm glad it did."

Natalie pulled away from him and shook her head. "Thank you for all the lovely gifts, but I think you'd better leave now."

Chase reached out and cupped her cheek in his palm. "Do you really want to marry this guy?"

She stiffened beneath his touch. "I made a promise to Edward and I intend to keep it."

Chase turned to the door, angry. "He doesn't deserve you," he muttered beneath his breath.

"And you do?" she demanded, her voice trembling. "Tell me, are you prepared to marry me? To give me a home and a future?"

"We barely know each other," he replied, his back still to her.

She stepped up beside him and grabbed his arm, forcing him to face her. "That's precisely right. We've known each other for less than twenty-four hours. And you want to destroy a relationship that's been part of my life for years. I'm not going to let you do that."

"Prove to me that you love him," Chase challenged. "Spend the day with me. I promise I won't try to kiss you again. I won't even touch you. But I can't let this go, Natalie."

"What right do you have to intrude on my life? Why are you doing this to me?"

"I don't know," Chase murmured, raking his fingers through his hair. "I wish I did. Maybe if we spend some time together, I'll be able to figure it out."

"No," she said, her chin set stubbornly.

"One day," Chase countered. "And then I'll walk away. I promise."

She closed her eyes and drew in a long breath. She wanted to refuse him, to push him out the door and make him go away. But a tiny voice inside her urged her to ignore common sense and appease her own curiosity. If she didn't, she'd be left to wonder about this man for the rest of her life. She couldn't allow this impetuous kiss to poison her happy future with Edward. "One day," Natalie finally agreed. "I'll spend one day with you and then you'll leave me in peace."

Reluctantly, Chase nodded.

"And no more kissing?"

Chase grinned. "I promise. For now, we're just friends."

SPRING HAD COME EARLY to the Northeast, the last weeks of March more lamb than lion. The snow and ice had given way to warm sun and cool rain, days that held all the promise of the summer to come. Traces of green sprang up in the most unlikely places, and Chase once again felt the lure of the sea, the same instinct that had tugged at his soul since childhood.

They had gathered up all the food in Natalie's foyer before they left and dropped it in the trunk of Chase's battered Porsche Speedster. Then, on a whim, he'd put the top down. Natalie had reluctantly climbed in, fearful of the cold but even more fearful of her prying neighbors. She'd spent the first part of their ride slouched down in the front seat, her hood pulled up to hide her face.

But now, as they raced along the old roads that connected tiny villages southeast of Boston, she pushed her hood back and turned her face up to the sun. Chase couldn't help but appreciate the sheer beauty of her blond hair whipping around her face, her eyes bright and her cheeks pink with cold. This day was more perfect than any in his memory and he wanted it to last forever.

Never mind the fact that he didn't know what the hell he was doing, speeding toward the sea with a woman who had promised herself to another man. All he knew was that it felt so right to be with her and he'd do anything in his power to make sure they'd be together again.

"You're beautiful," he called, taking his eyes off the road to get a long look at her. He wanted to reach over and touch her, to weave his fingers through the hair at her nape. But after the kiss they'd shared, he knew better than to push her. She was engaged and trying desperately to hold on to what she believed was her happiness. If he was patient, she would soon see that Edward was not the man for her.

"You shouldn't say things like that!" Natalie scolded.

"Why? It's the truth."

A blush crept up her cheeks and she gave him a hesitant smile, then shook her head. She seemed so uneasy with the compliment that he wondered if Edward had ever taken the time to flatter her.

"Where are we going?" she called above the wind.

"Someplace special."

She accepted his explanation without question, then continued to watch as the landscape turned from wide fields and forests to the flat sandy land that edged the Atlantic. Sand Harbor lay nestled on the western shore of Cape Cod Bay, a tiny seaside village off the same highway that wound its way to the very end of the peninsula.

Chase had chosen to live in Sand Harbor more for the snug marina than for its proximity to Boston. He'd purchased a small cottage near the water, and when he wasn't off on one of his sailing adventures, he settled into a quiet life, doing most of his business from home.

But he wasn't anxious to show Natalie the little house on Cape Street. Instead, he turned the car toward the waterfront and the tangle of ramshackle piers and crumbling quays. He stopped the Speedster in front of a chain-link fence, then hopped out and circled the car to open Natalie's door. He held out his hand to help her out, but she deliberately avoided his touch.

''This is someplace special?'' she asked.

''Be patient.'' Chase popped open the trunk and grabbed the bags of food, then slammed it shut with his elbow. He walked to the gate, Natalie at his heels, then fumbled with a rusty old padlock. The gate creaked open and she followed him inside.

''What is this place?''

''It's a boatyard,'' Chase said. ''And right there is my boat. The *Summer Day.*''

Natalie stared straight ahead at the thirty-five-foot sloop, its hull held aloft in a wooden cradle.

''I thought we'd have our picnic here. If the weather were warmer, I'd sail you to some secluded beach, but for now, this will have to do. I've still got to paint the hull before I put her in for the season.''

''I—I've never been on a boat before. I've always been afraid I'd get sick.''

Chase laughed. ''Well, there's no chance of that here.'' He placed the sacks of food on the ground, then grabbed a ladder, tipped it up and rested it on the gunwale. ''You go on up and I'll hand you the food.''

When he'd settled Natalie and their picnic supplies in the cockpit, Chase climbed down into the cabin and retrieved a pair of wineglasses and a corkscrew. When he returned, Natalie had crawled up to the bow and was standing there, the wind in her hair, staring out toward the harbor.

He watched her for a long time, recalling the dream that had sent her to him. Except for the jacket and the jeans, she looked exactly like he remembered. She looked like she belonged here with him.... The truth of Nana Tonya's prediction became more real with every second he spent with Natalie.

"You're the first woman I've ever had on my boat," he called. "Except for my grandmother."

Natalie turned and smiled at him, brushing hair out of her eyes. "I find that hard to believe," she teased. "According to office gossip, you're the type who always has a woman on your arm."

"But never on my boat," he said. "When I sail, I want to be alone."

She started back toward the cockpit, grabbing the shrouds for balance. "Then why did you bring me here?"

"Because you belong here. You've been here before."

She gave him a skeptical look but let it pass. "It sounds like your boat means a lot to you."

Natalie sat down and he poured her a glass of wine. "Most guys save up for a car," Chase said, "but not me. When I was a kid, I put my pennies away for a boat. I bought this one when I was sixteen. It was a mess, barely able to float. I worked on her for six years, every day of my summer vacation. The summer I graduated from college, I sailed her down the East Coast to the Carolinas. I promised to come back and take a job with the company, but I just kept sailing. For three years."

"How did you live?"

"Odd jobs, here and there."

"So you just ran away from life, from your responsibilities?"

"I embraced life and all its possibilities," Chase said.

Natalie looked out over the boatyard and sighed. "When I was younger, after my parents died, I used to dream about running away, about leaving all my problems behind and starting a brand-new life as a different person."

"What's stopping you now?"

"I've grown up," she said. "I have commitments—a career, a relationship, a new family. Stability and security. That's what I want. And that's what I'll have."

"And these things will make you happy?"

"I think so. I'm not sure. I've never had them before."

Chase leaned back and swirled the wine around in his glass, watching the sunlight glint through it. "I think you're selling life short, Natalie. You strike me as a woman who would enjoy a little adventure. A little danger."

"You're seeing only what you want to see," she murmured. "You don't know me at all."

Chase looked at her long and hard, trying to find the truth in her words. But even if she'd managed to fool herself, she couldn't fool him. Natalie Hillyard was not as she appeared. Chase sensed that there was a very different woman hiding behind her composed facade. An endlessly fascinating woman he was determined to discover.

THE DAY PASSED SO QUICKLY that Natalie was surprised to see the sun slipping below the horizon. A light lunch and a half bottle of wine had given her a warm, contented feeling she was reluctant to abandon. But she had given Chase his one day and that day was fast fading.

She had expected to feel relief, satisfaction that he'd finally be out of her life for good. But all she could muster was a sense of regret, a twinge of doubt and the fear that she might never feel so at ease again. Chase was fun; he laughed and teased and made her feel special. He told her silly stories and took pleasure in her reactions. So many times during the afternoon she'd looked up to find him watching her, his eyes slowly taking in every detail of her face, as if he were trying to commit it to memory.

But she didn't want the time they spent together to be just a memory. She wanted to hang on to it, like a lifeline; to have something to savor, if happiness somehow eluded her.

How could she have doubts? She'd made her choice and her choice was Edward. Yet a man she'd known for barely two days had thrown her life into chaos. Did she love Edward? Or was she merely settling for what she believed she wanted, as Chase predicted.

Chase Donnelly wasn't at all what she had expected. Office gossip had painted a rather overblown picture of a degenerate playboy bent on seduction. He seemed to take great amusement in that perception, constantly baiting her until she wasn't sure whether he was testing her or teasing her. But in the end, he'd let down his guard and shown himself to be a sweet and considerate man.

But what was it that *he* wanted? Was his passion for her so strong that he was willing to ignore her engagement? She'd never thought herself capable of eliciting such feelings from a man. But then, she'd never met a man like Chase before.

"Are you ready to go?"

She glanced up and smiled. His hair, blown by the wind, fell around his face and he brushed it back, then held out his hand. "For your first time on a sailboat, I'd say you did very well. Next time, we'll have to try it with the boat in the water."

There won't be a next time, she wanted to say. But she couldn't put her thought into words. She wanted to believe that she'd be happy; she wanted to know that there would be more beautiful spring days just like this. But she feared that Edward might never be able to give them to her.

"I should get back," she murmured, shoving her hands in her jacket pockets. "It's getting late."

Chase helped her down the ladder, taking care to touch her only when necessary. But she couldn't ignore the feel of his hand splayed across the small of her back as she made her way down, his warm fingers burning through her clothing to imprint on her skin.

They drove back the way they'd come, but this time Chase put the top up. Without the sound of the wind to distract her, the ride was filled with an uneasy silence. Natalie crossed her arms over her chest and sank down in the seat, a cold shiver pulsing through her body. With every mile that passed, a slow dread sank more deeply into her consciousness.

She was making the right decision. How could she possibly walk out on a marriage to a stable, reliable man for some sailor whose grandmother had had a vision? She would have to be crazy. Besides, what did she really know about Chase, beyond the stories that he'd told her about his childhood and the rumors that circulated at the office?

The two of them were polar opposites. He preferred to live his life without a plan, taking off for parts unknown at the slightest whim. She preferred a comfortable routine. He believed in destiny, in a silly dream that his grandmother had foretold. And she believed in practicality. No two people could be further apart in temperament and ideology than Natalie Hillyard and Chase Donnelly.

''I had a nice time today,'' she said, glancing over at him.

He smiled, but kept his eyes on the road, the passing cars bathing his features in white light and shadow. ''So did I. I'm glad we got a chance to know each other a little better.''

''And lunch. The food was wonderful.''

''Only The Best. That's the name of my business. We import gourmet foods, a lot of French wines, cheeses. The perfect business for someone who enjoys eating.''

"Edward is a banker," Natalie said, regretting her statement the moment it came out of her mouth.

She could see Chase's jaw tighten in the dim light from the dashboard. "Sounds boring."

She smiled, then shrugged her shoulders. "Yeah, I guess it is. He likes money, so it's a perfect job for him. And his father is a banker. Family tradition. The whole family loves money."

"And do you love him?" Chase asked. "Or the money?"

She heard the challenge in his voice, but decided to ignore it. "I've never really had much money until recently." Natalie bit her lower lip. "As for Edward, we're right for each other."

"You're sure of that?"

"I don't want this day to end with an argument," she said softly.

They passed the rest of the ride in silence, Natalie's mind whirling with confusion and doubt. She was almost relieved when Chase pulled up in front of the house on Birch Street. She would have preferred to get out of the car alone, but he hopped out and opened her door for her. He walked her to the front steps, stopping to stand in the shadows of the porch as she fumbled in her pocket for her keys.

When she finally found them, she looked up at Chase and forced a smile. "So, I guess this is goodbye." Natalie tried to make out his expression, but his features were hidden by the darkness. "Thank you—for today. And I—I hope you find the woman you're looking for."

His voice was soft, drifting out of the darkness. ''I already have.''

She wanted to turn and run inside, but she couldn't just leave him like that. ''I—I can't be that woman, Chase. I'm sorry. I hope you understand.''

He reached up to touch her and she stepped back. But slowly he brought his hand closer to her cheek, so close she could feel the warmth radiating from his skin. Still he didn't touch her.

''I would kiss you if I could,'' Chase murmured.

''But you can't.''

He brought his other hand up, but again he didn't touch her. ''I would hold your beautiful face in my hands, like this. And I'd bring my mouth down on yours. And you would taste so sweet and warm.''

Natalie shivered and instinctively turned her face into his hand, but he drew it away before their skin made contact.

Then, he bent slowly, until his mouth hovered over hers, until she could feel his breath on her lips. ''And as I kissed you, I'd pull your body against mine. You'd fit perfectly, every soft curve made just for me.''

''Chase, please.'' Her words came out in a strangled plea, but she didn't want him to stop.

''And after I had learned every inch of your body by heart, I'd make love to you. We would be so good together, Natalie. So perfect for each other.''

She reached up to place her fingers over his lips, to stop him from driving her mad with such talk. But he turned his head away. She could see his profile in the dim light from the streetlamps. His expression was cool and distant, filled with icy control.

She let her hand drop to her side, then closed her eyes. "I wish I could be more like you. More impulsive, more impetuous. If I was, I would kiss you right now. And we would walk up to my bedroom and we would make love to each other. But that's not who I am, Chase."

"How do you know? How will you ever know if you allow yourself to settle for this life you've constructed?"

"You don't understand. There are plans and invitations and gifts. It's too late."

"It's never too late," Chase said. "You've got the rest of your life ahead of you, Natalie. Are you willing to spend it with a man you don't love?"

Tears of frustration pushed at the corners of Natalie's eyes and she fought them with all her might. She wanted to shout at Chase, to slap his face and to scream that she *did* love Edward. But she'd known the truth for far too long and had simply chosen to ignore it, to believe that she would grow to love her husband over time.

Chase reached into his pocket and withdrew a business card, then pressed it into her hand. "If you ever need anything, night or day, I want you to call me. I promise to come, Natalie. Anytime, anywhere. All you have to do is call."

Natalie drew a shaky breath and slipped the card into her jacket pocket. "Goodbye, Chase." With that, she turned and hurried up the steps. Her hand shook as she shoved the key into the lock. By the time she'd gained the safety of the foyer, her whole body had begun to tremble.

''Put him out of your mind,'' she murmured to herself. ''You've made your decision and there's no going back now.''

Chapter Four

THE HOUSE ON BIRCH STREET was dark except for a single light illuminating a corner window on the second story. A crisp wind rustled the budding trees, and Chase tugged at the collar of his leather jacket to block the cold. He had stood in this same spot for the past three nights, staring at Natalie's bedroom window until the light went out and she went to bed.

He had tried to stay away, but he'd been drawn here against all his resolve. Why couldn't he forget Natalie as easily as she'd forgotten him? She was going to marry her fiancé and nothing he could do or say would change her mind. Yet some deep-seated instinct told him that he had to stop her. Why?

Was he so certain that they were destined to be together? Or did she simply represent a challenge, a prize he desired, yet couldn't hope to attain? He had always expected that he'd fall in love someday, but he hadn't anticipated that it would knock him down like a runaway train. He wasn't even sure if he loved her, only that, in the farthest corners of his heart, he believed they deserved a chance to be together.

Had they met in a different place and a different time, he might have courted her slowly, letting love unfold at its own pace. But the clock was ticking and every hour that passed brought them both closer to an irreversible event—her marriage to Edward.

Chase ran his fingers through his hair, then leaned back against the hood of his car. What could he hope to offer her that Edward hadn't? Chase had lived his life avoiding responsibility. Perhaps if he held down a regular job, if he put some money in the bank and bought himself a few business suits, he might at least look the part. But the thought of spending every day behind a desk at Donnelly Enterprises brought a bad taste to his mouth.

Besides, office gossip was a difficult thing to overcome. He'd always been known as the black sheep in the family, the ne'er-do-well. Would they even give him a chance, or would he be doomed from the start? He'd fought so long and hard against the pull of his family's expectations that to give in now seemed like the ultimate hypocrisy.

With a curse, Chase turned to pull open the door of his Porsche. But he couldn't leave. He had to see her, to try once more. He started for the front door, but then took a detour around the corner of the house. The oak tree stood like a sentinel, the boughs nearly touching her bedroom window. Chase scrounged for a handful of acorns, then shinnied up the trunk.

When he was level with her bedroom, he pitched an acorn at the glass. It bounced off with a resounding ping and he waited. Three more acorns hit the window before he saw her silhouette against the lacy drapes. The curtains parted and Natalie peered out into the darkness.

He threw one more acorn to catch her attention, then waved. The window sash flew up and she bent over the sill and squinted into the darkness. "Chase?" Her voice was soft on the chill wind and sent a current of desire shooting through him. "What are you doing out there?"

"We have to talk," he said, sliding out on a branch until he sat in a patch of light from the bedroom window.

"Why didn't you just ring the doorbell?"

"Because I knew that when you answered I'd have to pull you into my arms and kiss you. I've been thinking about you, Natalie. I can't stop thinking about you."

She sighed. "You *have* to stop."

Chase straddled the bough and slid closer to her. "And I've been thinking about making a few changes. About settling down and taking life a little more seriously."

Natalie smiled ruefully. "That's funny. Because I've been thinking that I take life far *too* seriously. Maybe you're the one who has it right and I've got it wrong."

"I could change. If I had a good enough reason."

She shook her head, her hair tumbling around her face. His fingers clenched as he imagined the silken feel of it, the sweet smell.

"I don't want you to change, Chase. Especially not for me. I spent my life becoming the person I am. Edward understands me and I understand him. There won't be any surprises between us. It will be all right, I promise.''

Chase swore softly. ''And when you kiss Edward, what do you feel, Natalie? When he touches you, does he set your blood on fire?''

''Passion isn't all there is to a marriage.''

''Then tell me how you felt when I touched you. Be honest with yourself.''

''I—I felt regret,'' she said. ''Regret that I'd broken Edward's trust.'' She paused. ''Regret that I hadn't met you years ago. With you, I might have become a different person.''

Chase inched a little farther out on the branch, close enough that he could look into her eyes. ''I think I love you, Natalie.''

Her eyes went wide and she shook her head. ''You don't even know me.''

''I know that you can't marry Edward.''

''We've had this discussion before,'' she warned.

Frustrated, Chase pushed out to the end of the bough. He was about to speak when a sharp crack sounded. Slowly, the branch gave way beneath him and he dropped like deadweight to the grass below.

Natalie screamed his name, but all he could hear was the sound of his breath being forced from his body. He tried to draw another, but the wind had been knocked out of him. Flat on his back, Chase closed his eyes and forced air into his lungs.

By the time Natalie reached his side, he'd managed to draw a few deep drafts of cold night air, restoring his health but severely damaging his pride.

"Are you all right?" she cried, taking his face between her palms and staring deeply into his eyes. "Lie still. Let me look at you."

Chase did as he was told, savoring the feel of her warm fingers on his face. He groaned as she bent over him and slowly ran her hands down his body, limb by limb. Her touch sent his senses reeling.

"Is anything broken? Where does it hurt? Did you hit your head?"

"I'm fine," he growled, trying to ignore the flood of desire that had pooled in the vicinity of his lap. She had no idea what she was doing to him. And no idea what he wanted to do to her.

Grabbing her around the waist, he tumbled her beneath him, stretching his body over hers and pinning her hands above her head. She twisted and wriggled, but her efforts to get away were feeble at best, her rhythmic movements becoming less unconscious and more deliberate with every second that passed.

"Let me go," she murmured, arching up against him, driving him mad with need.

He bent closer, his mouth nearly touching hers. "Do you really want me to?"

Her lips parted and her breath came in short gasps. He could hear the pounding of his own pulse and he fought for control. Had she just given him a sign, one word, he would have taken her right there on the lawn. But a flash of light against the house caught his attention.

Chase turned to see a police car slowly patroling the street. A spotlight glowed from near the driver's window and he cursed, then rolled off Natalie into the shadow of a large bush.

Natalie struggled to her feet, then brushed the dead grass and leaves from her damp nightgown. From Chase's vantage point behind her, the patrolman's light shone through the thin fabric, outlining her long legs and the soft curve of her hips, the spot where her thighs met. Chase smiled to himself as she waved to the police car, the sweet flesh of her breasts pressing against the nearly transparent fabric.

A voice boomed out of the darkness. ''Miss Hillyard? Are you all right?''

Natalie crossed her arms over her chest, giving Chase a deeper appreciation of her backside. ''I'm fine. I thought I heard a prowler, but it was just a stray dog. Nothing to worry about.''

Chase reached out and grabbed at her ankle, growling softly. With a quiet oath, she pulled away, then stomped on his fingers for good measure.

''Would you like me to take a look around?'' the patrolman called.

''No, everything is just fine. I'm fine, we're all fine here. Good night.''

They both watched as the policeman slowly continued his patrol of Birch Street and greater Redmond. When the car was finally out of sight, Natalie bent down and grabbed the collar of Chase's jacket. ''I want you out of my bushes and out of my life. Go home, Chase Donnelly. Now!''

He grinned and grabbed her hand, then kissed her palm. ''I'm in love with you, Natalie.''

"I said, go home. Get a good night's sleep. I'm sure you'll feel differently in the morning." With that, she lifted the damp hem of her nightgown and made for the front door.

Chase rolled on his back and stared up at the sky. "You're starting to like me, Natalie Hillyard," he called. "I can tell. It won't be long now."

"Go home!" she shouted.

Chase chuckled, the pushed himself to his feet. He brushed the damp earth from his jacket and jeans, then whistled a cheery tune as he walked toward his car. All and all, he'd had a fairly decent night. He'd told Natalie that he loved her and she'd once again told him to leave her alone.

But there was something in her tone that gave him hope. A little chink had appeared in the armor that she wore with such brazen determination. If he were a betting man, he'd have to lay money on the notion that Natalie Hillyard was starting to fall in love with him as well.

"A SILVER CHAFING DISH!" Natalie cried. "Mother Jennings, this is exactly what I wanted."

"A proper wife can never have too many chafing dishes," Mrs. Jennings intoned. Edward's elderly aunts and his cousins agreed, examining the fine silver as it was passed around the room. For Natalie's part, she wasn't sure what on earth she'd do with six silver chafing dishes, but she suspected she'd find out soon enough.

"I've never seen so much silver in my life," Lydia

muttered from her place next to Natalie on the sofa. "But where's the silver toilet brush? And the silver monkey wrench? Surely you put that on your list of must-haves."

"Stop it," Natalie whispered. "They'll hear you."

Lydia snorted in disgust. "Let 'em. If you ask me, they're all a bunch of uptight biddies with nothing better to do than nose around in your life."

Natalie pushed up from the sofa and smoothed her skirt. "If you bid—" She cleared her throat. "If you *ladies* will excuse me, I'll be back in a moment." Lydia stood up to follow, but Natalie waved her off. "Mother Jennings, why don't you tell Lydia all about that crystal vase we received from Edward's second cousin? Lydia adores fine crystal."

Lydia shot her a murderous look before Natalie slipped out of the room. She slowly wandered through the foyer to the rear of the house. To her relief, the powder room was empty and she closed the door firmly behind her.

Running her hands through her hair, Natalie stepped over to the mirror and glanced at her reflection. But the image that stared back at her took her by surprise. Her face was pale and drawn, lined with tension. She touched the corners of her mouth and attempted to smile, but all she could muster was a grimace.

To be honest, she hadn't felt any measure of happiness since the last time she'd seen Chase, four days ago. Her mind flashed back to that night beneath her bedroom window. Natalie slowly ran her hands along her body, trying to recall what it felt like to be beneath him, to feel his hard desire cradled against her hips.

The longer she stared into the mirror, the harder it was to recognize the woman staring back at her. "What am I doing?" Natalie whispered, reaching out to touch her reflection. "I don't belong here."

Suddenly, she couldn't remember how to breathe. Bracing her arms on the sink, Natalie bent over and tried to calm her racing heart. "I don't love him. And I don't want to marry him. And I certainly don't want to call that old battle-ax 'Mother.'"

Her gaze fell on the telephone above the toilet. She'd grown up in a house that had one phone. Edward lived in a house with a phone in every bathroom and two in the garage. Natalie snatched up the handset, then rummaged through her purse until she found her day planner. She flipped it open and slowly dialed Edward's number in London. It would be nearly eleven there. Edward always went to bed promptly at ten.

She just needed to hear his voice. That would calm her nerves and wash away the doubt that plagued her mind. He should never have left her so close to their wedding day. How was she expected to handle all the stress and the prewedding jitters on her own?

After three rings, he picked up.

"Edward?" Her voice cracked.

"Yes? This is Edward Jennings."

She nervously picked at a thread on her skirt. "Edward, it's Natalie."

He cleared his throat and she could imagine him sitting up in bed. "Natalie! Why are you calling?"

Natalie frowned. He sounded so cool and distant, the same way he sounded when she interrupted him at work. "I—I'm fine, Edward," She pressed her hand to her forehead and cursed. "Actually, I'm not fine."

"Natalie, can we talk some other time? I'm very busy right—"

"Edward, you were sleeping."

"Yes, well, I've had a long day and—"

Natalie took a long, deep breath. "Edward, I...I—"

"What?" he snapped. "What is it?"

She wasn't sure what possessed her at that very moment—whether it was his curt tone of voice or his reluctance to put her worries above his sleep. "I want to call off the wedding. I'm breaking our engagement. I can't marry you." A long silence hissed over their transatlantic connection as she waited for him to reply. "Edward? Are you there?"

"We'll talk about this when I get home," he said. "For now, I want you to calm down and consider your behavior. You're being irrational and impetuous. For God's sake, Natalie, grow up."

"I have considered my behavior," Natalie said stubbornly. "Believe me." She swallowed hard. "It's over, Edward. I'm sorry to tell you this by phone, but I can't go through with it. The wedding is off."

She waited, trying to still her trembling hand and her pounding heart. But he didn't say a word, didn't offer a protest or even a hint of surprise. Instead, she heard a click on the other end of the line and then, a few seconds later, a dial tone.

Natalie expected to feel some regret, some sadness.

But as she stood with the phone in her hand, the only thing she could muster was a surge of anger. She'd called him for comfort, for reassurance. And all he could give her was a few indifferent words and irritation at having his sleep interrupted.

She dropped the phone in its cradle and began to pace the perimeter of the bathroom, growing angrier by the second. "It's over," she murmured. "I've done it and it's over."

Beyond that fact, all she knew was that she had to get out of the Jenningses' house. Had she brought her own car, she would have ducked out the back and made an easy escape. But Mrs. Jennings had insisted on sending a car for her so that Natalie might have help when it came time to return home with her gifts.

"Lydia," Natalie murmured. "I'll take Lydia's car."

But Lydia was trapped in the parlor, listening to an endless diatribe about silver patterns and fine crystal and the proper way to clean a chandelier. There was no way to get a message to her without facing the rest of the guests and making up some lame excuse to leave. Natalie had never been a proficient liar.

She snatched up her day planner from the edge of the sink and rifled through it until she found the card she'd tucked inside. Anytime, he had told her. She punched out Chase's cell phone number, then said a silent prayer that he would answer. He picked up on the second ring.

Natalie swallowed hard and tried to calm her racing heart. "Chase? It's Natalie."

She closed her eyes and let the sound of his voice wash over her. ''I didn't think you'd call. God, Natalie, I've missed hearing your voice.''

''You said to call,'' she replied, ''if I needed you. And I do. I need you to come and get me. Right away. I'm in Redmond at 721 Kensington, right across from the square. Can you come?''

''I'm in the car now. I'll be there in fifteen minutes,'' he said.

Natalie let out a long breath, then smiled. ''Thank you.'' She hung the phone up, then sat down on the toilet to wait, nervously tapping her foot. The time ticked by on her watch and she tried to keep calm. Ten minutes had passed when she heard a knock on the door.

''Natalie? Are you in there?''

She opened the door a crack. The hallway was empty except for her sister, and Natalie quickly motioned her inside.

''What's going on?'' Lydia asked. ''Good grief, if I hear one more debate about the merits of sterling versus silver plate I think I'm going to tear my hair out. Are you all right?''

Natalie grabbed her sister and gave her a hug. ''I'm fine. I'm not going to marry Edward.'' She said it as easily as she might have commented on the weather.

Lydia gasped. ''What?''

''I've decided I can't marry Edward. I—I just called him and canceled the wedding.''

Lydia lowered herself to sit on the toilet, her mouth agape. ''When did you decide to do this?''

Natalie shrugged. "Just a few minutes ago. It hit me all at once. I can't marry him. This whole shower is for nothing."

"So are you going to hide out in the powder room until everyone goes home and Mrs. Jennings goes to bed? Or are you planning to make your big announcement before you leave?"

Natalie shook her head. "I called Chase. He'll be here in a few minutes."

"Chase Donnelly? You're leaving here with him?"

"If I can get out in one piece. I need you to go back into the parlor and keep everyone occupied. Especially Mother Jennings. I don't want to face her. Not yet." Natalie glanced at her watch again. "He should be here any minute. Go ahead. I'll be fine.

Lydia giggled. "I can't believe you, Nat. You're running out on your wedding and taking up with a man you barely know." She threw her arms around Natalie's neck. "Oh, I'm so proud of you."

Natalie returned her sister's hug, then opened the powder room door. "Go ahead. I'll call you tomorrow."

Lydia slipped out and Natalie waited a few minutes before she opened the small window above the toilet. She pushed out the storm window, then crawled up on the toilet and boosted herself into the opening. But either she had overestimated the size of the window or underestimated the size of her hips. Once she got halfway out, she could go no farther.

"Natalie? Are you in there?" Mother Jennings's

voice echoed in the hall and Natalie winced as she heard the powder room door open.

"Good God, Natalie, what are you doing?"

Natalie froze, wishing herself through the window and floundering in the bushes below. Anywhere but where she was. But there would be no quick escape, no easy way out. Natalie felt Mrs. Jennings tugging on her legs and she slowly slid back into the room.

"Explain yourself," Mrs. Jennings demanded. "What kind of behavior is this?"

Natalie straightened her suit jacket and tugged her skirt down from around her hips, then headed for the door, carefully avoiding Mother Jennings's considerable bulk. "I think you should call Edward," Natalie suggested. "He can explain."

"Explain? Explain what?"

"I—I just broke our engagement. I can't marry your son."

Mother Jennings followed her into the hallway, her florid face mottled with anger. "My dear, you can't be serious! The wedding is all planned. It's just a week away. The guests, the gifts, my reputation…!"

Natalie turned and faced her, her hands braced on her hips. "We'll call the guests and send back the gifts. I just can't do this."

Mrs. Jennings grabbed Natalie's elbow, her fingers biting into her flesh so hard that Natalie's eyes began to water. "Listen here. You will not embarrass this family. And you will not humiliate my son."

"I'm *thinking* of your son! I don't love Edward. I never have and I'm not sure I ever could. He's a very good man and he'll make someone a nice, dependable husband. But Edward and I don't belong together."

"You *will* marry my son," Mother Jennings threatened, "and I'll hear no more excuses."

Natalie was sure that Mrs. Jennings was about to slap her across the face, but she was saved by the sound of the doorbell. With a low growl, the older woman released Natalie's arm, pasted a tight smile on her face and hurried to the door. Her expression clouded with confusion when she saw Chase standing on the other side. "Who are you?"

"I'm here to pick up Natalie." Chase caught sight of her, then pushed past Mrs. Jennings and grabbed Natalie's hand. "Are you all right?"

Natalie nodded. "I'm ready to go now."

Chase led her to the door, keeping a careful eye on the older woman, who appeared ready to explode. "She looks mad," he murmured, bending close to Natalie's ear. "Who is she?"

"Edward's mother," Natalie whispered back. "Come on, let's get out of here."

He reached out and cupped her cheek in his palm. "Sweetheart, I'll take you wherever you want to go."

As he pulled the door shut behind him, Natalie heard Mother Jennings screech, "Sweetheart? Sweetheart? Did he call you sweetheart? Come back here, you impertinent little hussy!"

Then Natalie heard Chase's laugh, warm and rich and filled with delight, and she knew everything would be all right. As long as Chase was beside her, there was nothing she couldn't conquer.

Chapter Five

THE TIRES OF the Speedster squealed as Chase pulled away from the curb. He glanced over at Natalie, whose face was suddenly pale. Then he slid his hand across the back of her seat and slowly began to massage her neck. "Take a few deep breaths," he said. "You'll feel better in a minute. What happened in there?"

She did as she was told, her gaze fixed on the road ahead. When she finally spoke, her voice trembled. "I—I just called him up and told him I wasn't going to marry him. I've never done anything like that in my life!"

Chase yanked the wheel to the right and slammed on the brakes, the car skidding to a stop. He reached over and turned Natalie toward him, forcing her eyes to meet his. "You're not engaged anymore?"

Mutely she shook her head, her eyes wide with disbelief.

With a low growl, Chase pulled her into his arms and kissed her long and hard. Natalie wrapped her arms around his neck and, after the initial surprise, returned his kiss in full measure, her lips growing soft and pliant against his.

God, it felt good to lose himself in the sweet taste of her. For the past week, he'd thought of nothing else, though he'd been determined to put what they'd shared in the past. He'd even made plans to leave Boston, to take the *Summer Day* and sail her somewhere far away from memories of Natalie Hillyard.

Chase cupped her face in his hands, then slowly trailed kisses across her cheeks and over her eyes. Her lashes fluttered and she looked up at him and smiled. "Thank you for coming to my rescue."

"Anytime, anywhere, sweetheart."

Natalie blushed. "I like that, when you call me sweetheart."

Chase leaned back in his seat and braced his hands on the wheel. "Well, sweetheart, where should we go? This is your escape, so you need to tell me the plan."

Natalie blinked. "I—I'm not sure I have a plan. I guess I'm homeless. I can't live at the Birch Street house anymore. And my sister has a tiny studio apartment. I suppose I should find a hotel room somewhere."

Chase put the car in gear and glanced over his shoulder before pulling out into the street. "First we'll go back to the house and pick up a few of your things."

"I don't want to go back there," Natalie said, shaking her head.

Chase grabbed her hand and pressed her wrist to his lips. "It'll be all right. I'll go in with you."

The next few blocks passed in silence, then she suddenly turned to him, her expression creased with worry. "What do you think will happen?"

"Happen?"

"When Edward gets back. Do you think he'll be angry? He just hung up on me."

"What do you mean?"

"He didn't even put up a fight. He didn't tell me that he loved me. He wasn't even really upset. He just hung up."

"Any man who lets you go so easily doesn't deserve you."

"I didn't want to hurt him, Chase. None of this is his fault. Do you think he'll be able to forgive me... someday?"

Chase wished there was a way to calm her fears, to erase the regret that he knew she would feel. She'd been with Edward for most of her adult life, and whether they had loved each other or not, they had certainly shared some affection between them, an attachment strong enough to warrant marriage plans.

Chase cursed silently. This was all that he ever wanted—Natalie beside him, her fiancé a part of her past. But would she come to regret her decision? Would he be able to make her happy for the rest of her life? He wouldn't know unless he tried. And damn if he wouldn't try his very best.

"I think that, given time, Edward will realize you only wanted to find happiness."

"I am happy," Natalie said. "And scared. And relieved."

Five minutes later, they pulled up in front of the Birch Street house. Chase helped Natalie out of the car, then held tight to her hand as they walked up to the porch. But she stopped before they reached the front door and shook her head. "I don't want to go in there. Can't we just leave it like it is? I can buy new clothes."

Chase pulled her against him and kissed the top of her head, inhaling the sweet scent of her hair. "Why don't you wait out here and I'll gather up your things? It will only take a minute." She nodded and Chase took the keys from her hand and unlocked the door.

He found a suitcase under her bed and tipped her dresser drawers into it. Clothes from the closet followed, along with the contents of the bathroom's medicine chest. He wasn't sure what else to take, grabbing shoes from the rack and stuffing them into an overnight bag. When he'd packed all he could carry, he headed back down the stairs.

He found Natalie standing in the doorway, her gaze slowly taking in every detail of the foyer from just beyond the threshold. "I never liked this house," she murmured. "It always felt so cold and empty. So pretentious. I don't think it would have ever felt like a home."

"Come on," Chase said. "Let's get out of here. I'm taking you home."

"Home?"

"To my house in Sand Harbor. You can stay with me until you figure out what you want to do."

She placed her hand on his shoulder. "There's one more thing." Chase watched as she twisted the huge diamond ring off her finger. Then she handed it to him. "Would you put this on the table beneath the mirror? Edward always drops his keys there. He'll be sure to find it. Maybe he can take it back, or sell it...or give it to someone else.''

Chase set the suitcases on the floor and did as she asked. He had accomplished what he had set out to do. He'd stolen Natalie Hillyard away from her fiancé. The diamond glinted in the light from the doorway as if to remind him of his part in this drama.

He drew a deep breath, then turned back to Natalie. ''Ready?''

She took one last look around, then nodded. ''I guess there's no going back now.''

''No going back now,'' he murmured.

WITH EVERY MILE that passed, Natalie's life in the Birch Street house seemed to fade into the distance. The afternoon was warm and sunny, and Chase had put the top down on the Porsche. Natalie stared at the countryside as it flew by, her hair whipping at her face, the wind cold on her cheeks.

She felt free, unburdened, as if her life with Edward had never existed. She had put her faith in destiny and it had brought her to a crossroads. In the past, she had always chosen the safe route, traveling slowly and cautiously. But something had happened in that powder room at the Jenningses' house. A new road had appeared on the horizon and she had decided to follow it.

Natalie glanced over at Chase. She wasn't sure what would happen between them, but she wanted to find out. He'd promised her nothing except unbridled passion and unquestioned love. For now, that was enough.

The rest would follow. After all, he was her destiny, wasn't he?

Sand Harbor was not far from Redmond, but Natalie felt as though she'd traveled miles and miles. Chase maneuvered the car through narrow streets of picturesque cottages surrounded by picket fences. Then, without warning, he pulled the car over and switched off the ignition.

"This is it," he said. He jumped out of the car and opened her door, then went to grab her bags from the trunk. "I'm not sure how it looks inside. My cleaning lady hasn't been here for a while so you'll have to ignore the dust."

Natalie stopped on the narrow cobblestone walk and took a long look at Chase's house. It wasn't close to what she would have expected for a Donnelly. The entire house could have fit into a small corner of the mansion on Birch Street.

The Cape Cod cottage was sided in beautiful weathered wood, gray with age. A wide porch spanned the width of the facade, the blue trim creating a pretty contrast. And a garden on either side of the front steps lay ready to plant with spring flowers. The house was only a few blocks from the sea, and she could smell the salt tang in the air.

It was the house she'd always imagined in her dreams of happy endings. "It's perfect," Natalie said.

Chase pushed the key into the lock, then stepped aside to let her pass. "I like it. I don't have much need for anything bigger." He followed her inside, her bags in his arms, then kicked the door shut with his foot.

She slowly took in all the details of the charming interior—the comfortable furniture, the threadbare rugs...the huge bed that lay just beyond the bedroom door. Natalie finally turned to look at him, a hesitant smile on her lips. "I—I can't believe I broke the engagement."

"You're not engaged anymore," Chase murmured.

"No, I'm not engaged."

He met her gaze and held it for a long moment. Then, without blinking, he dropped her bags on the floor and crossed the room in three long strides.

Natalie met him halfway, throwing herself into his arms and meeting his mouth with all the desire they had denied for too long. The contact was instantly electric, stunning her with its intensity. He picked her up off her feet and held her tightly, then let her body slide down along his until her toes touched the floor.

Without breaking the kiss, Chase fumbled to push her jacket off. She twisted beneath his hands and tugged at the cuffs, then tossed it on the floor. Frantic fingers worked at buttons and zippers as Chase and Natalie tore at each other's clothes. Moments later, she was left in only her silk panties and camisole, Chase in his jeans, the top button undone.

She had frightened herself with this overwhelming desire that seemed to engulf her the instant his lips touched hers. He held such power over her, breaking down her inhibitions until nothing stood between them. With Chase, she had no past. Everything seemed as if she were experiencing it for the first time.

"I—I'm not very good at this," Natalie said, a tremor in her voice.

Chase stepped back and stared down into her eyes, running his fingers through her hair. Then he kissed her softly and smiled. "You just haven't been with the right man."

"Are you the right man?"

Playfully, Chase grabbed her around the waist, bunching the silk of her camisole in his fists. He tugged her closer until her hips met his, the hard ridge of his arousal rubbing against her stomach through the silk and denim barriers. A devilish grin curled his lips. "Sweetheart, from now on, I'm the only man."

A giggle bubbled up from Natalie's throat and she pressed her face against his naked chest, a warm blush burning her skin. His heart thudded strong and even beneath her cheek. "Then how do we start?"

"First we get rid of the rest of these clothes."

"Here?" she asked, glancing around the room.

"We'll start here." His fingers slipped beneath the straps of her silk camisole and tugged them over her shoulders. Natalie felt the fabric drift down her breasts. Instinctively, she drew her arms up to keep herself covered, but Chase grabbed her wrists to stop her. Gently, he lowered her arms, refusing to accept her reticence. The camisole slid over her hips and puddled on the floor at her feet.

"Now it's your turn," he said, taking a step back.

Natalie took a deep breath and tried to calm her racing heart. What if she did something wrong? She had never been a very active participant in this particular activity. Nor had she ever made love in broad daylight or outside the confines of a bedroom.

She reached for the waistband of his jeans and with shaking hands worked at the zipper. Her fingers brushed along his hard shaft and she heard him moan. Impatient, he pushed the denim over his hips, kicking off his shoes and socks along with the jeans.

He had a beautiful body, so lean and hard, with muscles rippling beneath taut, tan skin. His boxers rode low on his narrow hips, and Natalie's eyes followed the soft line of sun-burnished hair from his collarbone to beneath the waistband, drawing her attention to the blatant evidence of his desire.

Emboldened, she touched him, lightly stroking him through the soft fabric. There was power in what she did, for his breath quickened and he tipped his head back, a mixture of pleasure and pain crossing his handsome features.

Suddenly, he sucked in a sharp breath and grabbed her wrist to stop her. Chase drew her hand up along his chest, then placed a kiss on her palm, an unspoken signal that it was his turn to torment her. With exquisite tenderness, he explored her body with his mouth. Her head swam and her limbs went boneless with every new spot he discovered. And then his mouth was gone and she was in his arms as he carried her toward the bedroom.

She wanted to stop him, to tell him that she wasn't ready. But her body had betrayed her. She wanted something more, something she couldn't describe. It was so close, twisting at her core in unbearable anticipation. And she knew only he could satisfy her now.

They tumbled onto the bed, a mess of rumpled sheets and crushed pillows, the faint scent of his aftershave in the air. He pulled her up against him and slid his hand along her stomach until he reached the lace of her panties.

Natalie knew her release was there, beneath his touch, and she arched up, choosing to follow her instincts, her body craving more. His fingers found her moist core and he began to caress her. Desire twisted inside of her and she cried out as the tension became too much to bear. His name crossed her lips, over and over in a soft plea.

And then Natalie's breath caught in her throat and her body went still. Suddenly, she was there—breaking, falling, drowning as wave after wave of pure pleasure coursed through her every nerve, every vein. It wasn't supposed to feel so incredibly good, so unbearably right. But it did and it only left her craving more.

When her heart had calmed and her breath had stilled, she pushed herself up on her knees and looked down at him, at his beautiful body stretched out in the tangled sheets. She reached out and ran her palm along his chest, taking delight in the fact that she could do so without hesitation. At this moment, he belonged entirely to her. And she wanted him, body and soul. "Make love to me," she whispered.

He groaned, then pulled her over on top of him. Soft flesh met hard desire and Chase quickly removed the final barriers between them. He brought her thighs up along his hips and Natalie felt him beneath her, ripe and ready, his silken shaft probing at her entrance.

She had always known that this was the way it should be, so intense and so uninhibited, carnal pleasure the only thing that mattered. There was nothing she wouldn't do, no act too intimate. With her hand, she guided him inside of her, sinking down on top of him until she ached.

They moved together, slowly at first. But passion overwhelmed them both and restraint was far beyond their grasp. Before long, they were both near the edge, frantic with need, rocking against each other, striving for fulfillment. He called out her name, a plea for release, and she met him there, in a single, soul-shattering moment, a moment she had never known before.

Later, they made love again, this time slowly and gently, and to Natalie it was new all over again. She hadn't known how good it could be between a man and a woman, because she had never known Chase. He had uncovered a different side of her nature, a passion hidden within her. A passion that would be his and his alone.

CHASE WATCHED NATALIE from the bed, tucking his arm under his head for a better view. She had pulled a polo shirt from his dresser and tugged it over her head, covering her slender body above the delicious curves of her backside.

She wandered around the bedroom, staring at the

photos on the wall—sunsets, sailboat scenes, memories of his many trips around the world. "You've been to so many places," she murmured. "I've never traveled much."

He smiled as she bent, enjoying the tantalizing view. There were many places he wanted to take her, in the bedroom and in the world. "Then we'll have to change that. When you go into work on Monday I think you should arrange for a few weeks off. I want to take you on a vacation."

"But I couldn't," Natalie said. "I—"

"Why not? The day I came into the office, John told me that you never take time off. He told me that you and Edward didn't even plan to take a honeymoon."

"Edward hates..." She paused, a flush coloring her cheeks. "I mean, he hated vacations. He wasn't the type to relax."

"Well, I am. Where would you like to go? Tahiti, the Canaries? How about the Greek Isles?"

Natalie smiled winsomely, then crawled back into bed with him. She snuggled up against his body and threw her leg over his hips. "Why don't we stay right here? Two weeks together in bed. There are so many places I've yet to explore."

Chase growled and nuzzled her neck. "That sounds good to me. When do we take off?"

Suddenly, she sat up. "I'm famished. I don't think I've eaten in days. Can you cook?"

"Can *I* cook?"

Natalie pushed up on top of him and straddled his

hips, brushing her pale hair out of her eyes. "I guess you should know that I can't cook. As a wedding present, Mother Jennings was going to hire a housekeeper for me. So, unless you cook, we might not be eating very well."

Chase spanned her waist with his hands, then gently moved her until she could feel his growing erection beneath the sheets. Her eyes went wide and she sent him a lazy smile. "Right now, I'm not thinking about food," he murmured.

With a playful shove, she slipped off of him, then walked to his desk, tucked in a cozy alcove near the window. "I need some paper, I'll make a grocery list."

He groaned and rolled over on his side, the sheet slipping off his hips. "We can send out, Nat. Come back to bed."

"No, I want to cook dinner. It will be another new experience for me." She rummaged through the stacks of files and papers on his desk, then paused and picked up a copy of Donnelly Enterprises' corporate newsletter. "Did you read this issue?" she asked, showing him the cover.

"I read every issue," he grumbled. "Come back to bed."

She opened the newsletter and pointed to a huge picture in the center spread. "Here I am. I don't really like this photo. I thought it made me look too… feminine. Not very businesslike."

Chase pushed up in bed, staring across the room at the photograph of Natalie. "Can I see that?" He held out his hand and she shrugged, then crossed the room and gave him the newsletter. Flipping through the pages, he felt an odd worry niggling at the back of his brain.

"That's the most recent one," Natalie said. "It came out two or three weeks ago."

"I read this issue," he murmured. "And I remember reading the article about you."

She sat down on the edge of the bed and rested her chin on his shoulder, her gaze fixed on the open page. "That's strange that you read it and then you..." The words died in her throat and the color drained from her flushed cheeks.

"I read it," Chase said. "I saw your picture but it didn't really register...at the time." He drew in a deep breath, the worry coming into focus. "Or maybe it did." His jaw grew tight. "And then a few nights later, I dreamed about you."

Natalie pushed off the bed, her gaze still fixed on the photo. "Then—then it wasn't really destiny. You didn't dream of the woman you were going to marry. You dreamed of the woman you had just seen in the company newsletter."

Chase didn't know what to say. The instant he saw the picture, he had come to the very same conclusion. Nana Tonya had planted a seed in his mind and he had dreamed of a woman. But was she really the woman he was destined to marry? "It was you in the dream, Nat. Not someone else. That's all that really matters." He meant to ease her fears, but even he could hear the doubt in his voice.

She shook her head, her hair tumbling around her face in unruly waves. Slowly, she backed away from the bed. ''No, that's not right. This was supposed to be fate. You made me believe it.''

Chase slipped from the bed, grabbing the sheet to wrap around his waist. ''So what if it wasn't? We're together. We're happy. And I love you.''

''Do you?'' she challenged. ''Or do you just think you do? Have you managed to *convince* yourself that you love me because of some silly illusion your grandmother put in your head? You can't tell me that this doesn't cause a little doubt, can you?''

Chase reached out and took her hand. ''All right, maybe it has thrown me off. But forget about the dream, about my grandmother's prediction. Think about us, together. Think about what we share. Who we are.''

Closing her eyes, she yanked her fingers from his and pressed her palms together beneath her chin. Then she met his gaze squarely. ''I knew who I was. And I knew exactly what I wanted, until you came along and convinced me differently. Why couldn't you have left well enough alone?''

''Dammit, Nat, this shouldn't make a difference.''

''Look at me and tell me that you believe that. That you aren't thinking that maybe this whole destiny thing is a load of crap.''

He couldn't tell her that; he couldn't lie to her. He'd believed it as surely as she had, even more so. He'd allowed it to color his judgment, to override his common sense. He'd been carried away on a dream that really wasn't a dream at all. And now reality was crashing in all around them and he didn't know how to stop it. "We just need time," Chase murmured. "Time to think."

"This was all a mistake. Maybe I *was* supposed to marry Edward all along."

Chase swore out loud. "You can't believe that, Natalie. Not after what we just shared."

"But how do you know?" Her voice trembled with emotion and Chase saw tears well in her eyes. "You can't be sure. No more than I can." With a weak sob, she bent and hurriedly picked up her clothes, scattered about the floor. "I—I have to get out of here. I have to find a quiet place to sort this all out."

Chase reached out for her, but she evaded his hand. "Natalie, you don't have to leave. This is something we need to work out together."

"I believed you," she cried. "I really believed that we were destined for each other, even though I never believed in fate before. And now I find out that this was all a mistake. How could I have been so gullible?"

"This was not a mistake!"

She pulled her jacket on over her badly buttoned silk blouse, then snatched her shoes from the floor. "I didn't think," she said, pressing her palms to her temples. "Something strange happened to me when we met and I just...went crazy. I'm not this person. I'm not someone who acts on impulse, someone who jumps into bed at the slightest whim. I—I'm not...a passionate person."

Chase followed her to the door, reaching out to grab her by the arm. "Don't leave. We can talk this out."

She pulled out of his grasp and flung the door open. "I can't talk right now. I have to think." Without looking back, she stumbled down the front porch steps and headed toward the waterfront.

"Natalie, wait! I'll get dressed and come with you."

She didn't look back. "I need to be alone."

Chase closed his eyes and tipped his head back. What the hell had happened here? Everything had finally been settled between them, and now this! Sure, he'd seen her before. But did that really mean that his dream had been a mistake? He couldn't deny the momentary sliver of doubt he'd felt upon seeing her photo. But that was far overpowered by the love he felt for Natalie.

They belonged together, didn't they? He'd never experienced such intense attraction, such overwhelming desire until he'd met her. She'd become a part of his future, and he'd known since the moment he stepped into the elevator that he would someday marry her.

But how much of that certainty had been based on his grandmother's prediction and his subsequent dream? And how much was grounded in reality? Had Natalie always been there, deep in his subconscious, just waiting to pop up in a dream? Chase leaned back against the weathered clapboard siding of his house and pressed the heel of his hand to his forehead, his eyes still pinched shut.

"Is that a sheet you're wearing?"

Chase's eyes snapped open, and to his shock, he

found his grandmother staring up at him from the bottom of the porch steps. "Nana Tonya! What are you doing here?"

"I am preventing you from being arrested for indecent exposure, perhaps?"

Glancing down, Chase saw that the sheet had slipped precariously low on his hips. With a sheepish smile, he tugged it back up. "Sorry. I was..."

"In bed? In the middle of the day?"

"Don't ask questions. I shouldn't have to explain my sex life to my grandmother." He pushed open the front door. "Besides, you're the one who has some explaining to do."

"Me?"

"Why don't we go inside? You can tell me why you're here. And I don't want to hear that you've had another one of your visions."

Nana stepped into the living room, then tugged off her gloves impatiently. "I am here because you invited me to have dinner with you. And I arrive and find that you have been—" she shook her head "—doing the wild thing, is that how you say it?"

Chase couldn't help but laugh, not just at her comment, but at the charming humor that her accent added. "You better not say a word, Nana. This was all your fault."

"Your sex life is my fault? Now this is news to me."

"The dream," Chase said. "Remember your vision? Well, it came true. That very night, the night of your birthday party, I dreamed of a beautiful woman. And the next day, I came face-to-face with her.''

Nana Tonya pressed her palm against her heart. ''This is true? You have met the woman you are going to marry?''

''I thought I did. Hell, I even had a hand in breaking up her engagement to another man. But then, right before you got here, things got a little messed up. Destiny isn't all it's cracked up to be.''

Nana took a step forward and craned her neck to see into the bedroom. ''She is still here?''

''No. She went out for a walk. You see, we discovered that she didn't just appear in my dream. I'd seen her before. At least, a picture of her, in the company newsletter.''

''And this is a problem? Why?''

''Because it means that fate didn't have a hand in my dream.''

Nana waved her hand and clucked her tongue. ''But you love her, don't you?''

He had impulsively said the words to Natalie before, and had just as quickly doubted their truth moments ago. But he had never examined the real depth of his feelings. After a moment's reflection, he had his answer. ''Yes, I do love her. I fell in love with her the moment I saw her.''

His grandmother stepped toward him and poked her finger into his chest. ''Then what is all this doubt? You love the woman and I would assume she has feelings for you. Why are you standing here talking to your Nana Tonya when you should be out looking for her?''

Chase stared down at her, shaking his head in bemusement. Nana Tonya had an uncanny knack for cutting right to the chase. He planted a kiss on top of her head, then patted her cheek. ''I think that's exactly what I'll do.''

Chapter Six

SHE HAD ASKED FOR TIME—time to think, to sort out the jumble of emotions that had tossed her life into chaos. Chase had found her that day, sitting on a park bench overlooking the harbor, and they had talked. But in the end, she still couldn't bring herself to believe that nothing had changed between them. So, he'd driven her—and her luggage—to her sister's.

Couldn't he see that everything had changed? She had placed her trust in fate, in the dream that they truly belonged together. She'd ignored her common sense and logic, two characteristics that she'd come to depend on during her lifetime. Natalie Hillyard did not take risks. She did not act impetuously or irrationally. And she certainly didn't fall in love with a man she barely knew.

Natalie stared out her office window, watching the twinkling lights of the city night through a dreary drizzle. This was where her impetuousness had led. She didn't have Edward; she didn't want Chase. She was all alone again, abandoned exactly as she'd been twenty years ago, as far away as ever from finding the security and the family that she'd always longed for.

She'd found it, for a short time, with Edward—only she hadn't loved him. And then she'd found it again with Chase—only she hadn't trusted him.

Natalie closed her tired eyes and rubbed her forehead, trying to massage away the tension. She had hoped to occupy her mind with work, but her thoughts constantly returned to Chase, to that flicker of doubt she'd seen in his eyes, to his uneasy attempts to calm her fears. If he wasn't sure, then how could she be?

Sighing in frustration, Natalie pushed away from her desk and crossed her office to retrieve her coat from behind the door. Though she didn't want to go back to Lydia's tiny apartment, to her sister's curious looks and sympathetic comments, she couldn't stay in the office any longer. She flipped off her light, then made her way through the darkened lobby to the elevator.

"You work very hard."

Natalie jumped in surprise, her hand flying to her chest. She glanced around the reception area, her gaze stopping on an elderly woman who sat primly in one of the guest chairs. She slowly stood, leaning heavily on her cane, then held out her hand.

"I am sorry to have startled you," she said, her soft voice lilting with an unfamiliar accent. "But I needed to speak to you."

Natalie glanced around the office. The door had been locked, the security guard vigilant. How had this woman gotten in at such a late hour? "I'm on my way home. If you have business with the company, you can make an appointment during business hours."

"I came here to see you, Miss Hillyard."

"Miss Hillyard?" Natalie frowned. "How did you know my name?"

"I'm Antonia Donnelly," she replied. "Nana Tonya?"

Natalie gasped. Antonia Donnelly was the majority stockholder in Donnelly Enterprises, the matriarch of the Donnelly clan. And Nana Tonya was Chase's Gypsy grandmother. Natalie hadn't realized until this moment that they were one and the same. "Mrs. Donnelly, it's a pleasure to meet you," she said, taking her hand. "What can I do for you?"

"I hoped that we would have a chance to talk. I have my car downstairs. May I offer you a ride home?"

"Of course." Natalie walked beside the older woman to the elevator, then stood silently as they rode down to the street level. "I'm staying with my sister. She lives near Boston College. It's not far."

"This elevator," Antonia said softly, looking around. "This is where you met Chase, isn't it?"

Natalie glanced at her, shocked by her psychic powers. Antonia chuckled and waved her hand. "Do not look at me like that. Chase told me all about it. There is only one other elevator, so I had a fifty-fifty chance."

"He told me you have these...visions."

"Hmm," she said, nodding. "I told him he would dream of the woman he would marry, and he dreamed of you. And now you are unhappy."

"He'd already seen my picture. That's why he dreamed of me. It wasn't anything magical at all."

Antonia shrugged. "That is of no consequence. He

still dreamed of you. My vision was correct. I'm rarely wrong, you know.''

''Rarely?'' Natalie asked.

The woman reached out and patted Natalie's arm. ''Presidential elections and pro football. I can't seem to get a fix on those. But I am quite good with the ponies, my grandson tells me.''

The elevator doors opened and they walked out into the brightly lit lobby. The security guard nodded as they passed, wishing Antonia a good night with easy familiarity. Outside, her driver waited, umbrella at the ready, to escort them to the car parked at the curb.

''Come,'' Antonia said. ''I will take you wherever you want to go. But first, we will have tea.''

Natalie crawled in the back seat of the car after Antonia, then settled herself, brushing the rain off her coat. The car pulled into traffic as Antonia tugged off her gloves. ''I was quite anxious to speak with you. After my vision, I have been curious.''

''Mrs. Donnelly, I really don't—''

''Believe in my visions? Chase told me that. But I still felt it was important to speak with you. I was watering my houseplants this afternoon and contemplating a very sad looking African violet when I saw you. You were asleep on a sofa bed in a tiny apartment.''

''I—I am staying at my—''

Antonia stopped her again with another wave of her hand. ''I know. You are staying with your sister. Her name is...Lydia. An art student?''

''But how did you—''

"Chase told me."

Natalie leaned back against the plush leather seat. Was she really to believe in Antonia Donnelly's powers? Or should she merely humor an old woman who listened very closely to every bit of information her grandson offered? "When I called off my wedding yesterday, I became homeless," Natalie explained. "I need to look for an apartment of my own."

"You should be living with my grandson," Antonia said, slapping her gloves against her palm. "You would be happy with him. I can see it already."

"Another prediction?" Natalie asked.

"No," she replied. "I simply know my grandson and how he feels about you. He would make you happy—this, I know. And you would have very pretty babies together. I would like to be a great-grandmama."

Natalie shifted uneasily. "I don't think Chase and I are really meant for each other. We're so different."

"This is good!" she cried. "My husband and I were very different. And we loved each other deeply. Being the same is not always good. Different is better."

"Is that why you came here?" Natalie asked. "To try to convince me to go back to Chase?"

"I came here to convince you that it would be foolish to ignore your feelings for him." Antonia leaned forward. "Winston, take us to that drive-through restaurant that I like, the one with the big dinosaur out front. We'll have a nice cup of tea and some cookies. Would you like that, dear?"

Natalie sighed and nodded. A few minutes later,

they were sipping tea from plastic cups and munching on dinosaur cookies in the parking lot of a fast-food restaurant. Antonia chattered on about Chase, relating story after story from his childhood until Natalie felt as if she'd known him for years.

Antonia didn't make another attempt to convince Natalie of the truth of her vision, nor did she urge Natalie to return to Chase. Instead, she enumerated the qualities that would make her grandson a good husband.

The last time Natalie had talked to Chase, he had promised to give her some time to think, and she planned to take all the time she needed to sort out her confusion. Had he sent his grandmother, instead, to plead his case? Though Natalie wanted to believe he might do such a thing, she got the feeling that Nana Tonya had come of her own accord.

When they finally arrived in front of Lydia's building, Antonia reached out and took Natalie's hand. ''It does not matter how you come to love,'' she said. ''It only matters that you love at all.''

Natalie bent closer and gave Antonia a kiss on the cheek. For a moment, the woman went still and then she blinked. ''Tonight you will dream of your wedding day,'' she murmured.

Stunned by Antonia's odd behavior, Natalie mumbled her goodbyes and then hurried out of the car. She ran toward the lobby of Lydia's building, then turned around and watched as the car drove off. A cold shiver skittered down her spine and she tugged her collar up against the rain before she headed inside.

Later that night, she couldn't sleep for fear of what awaited her on the other side of consciousness. She lay on Lydia's sofa bed, fighting off her exhaustion by doing complex multiplication problems in her head. And when she finally drifted off, sometime before dawn, she dreamed of her wedding.

Dressed in white, she slowly walked down the aisle. Through a haze, she saw Edward waiting for her, and nearby, his mother and father watched. But as she walked toward him, a wind whipped through the open windows of the church, clearing away the fog. Swirling around her, the breeze caught her veil, lifting it from her head to float above her like a cloud. She tried to catch it, jumping up until the tulle brushed her fingers. But it was just out of her reach. She couldn't get married without a veil. She couldn't…she couldn't….

Natalie woke up breathless, staring up at the ceiling with unblinking eyes. Her heart twisted and she moaned softly as a shiver of apprehension coursed through her. Antonia Donnelly had been right—she'd dreamed of her wedding. But Natalie hadn't dreamed of Chase, she'd dreamed of Edward.

Edward…the man she'd been destined to marry all along. Her breath caught in her throat. How had she managed to mess up her life so thoroughly? And why had she allowed a man like Chase to push her off course?

Natalie rolled over and punched her pillow. Tomorrow she would set everything to rights. Tomorrow, she'd get her life back on track.

"I WAS UNDER A LOT of pressure. After all, nothing in my experience prepared me for the...social obligations, the responsibilities. But I'm hoping that you'll be able to forgive my behavior. My lapse in judgment."

Natalie calmly folded her hands on her desk, then looked at Edward and his mother. She had never expected that Edward would accept her invitation to talk, much less bring his mother along. But the pair had been waiting in her office when she arrived on Wednesday morning.

She'd had a stilted conversation with Edward late Tuesday night after he'd arrived back home at the Birch Street house, and they'd agreed to get together later in the week to clear up the return of the wedding and shower gifts. In a small corner of her mind, she hoped that he might find a way to forgive her.

Mrs. Jennings cleared her throat. "I certainly am not going to ask you what prompted this sudden change in your behavior, though I have my suspicions."

Natalie knew Edward's mother was referring to Chase, and she wondered how much of Sunday's events had been relayed to Edward. After all that had happened, the last thing she wanted to explain was her crazy attraction to a wholly unsuitable man. A momentary lapse, that's what it had been. And that she'd actually believed their short relationship was destiny—well, that was too embarrassing to think about.

She had put Chase and their crazy affair in perspective—and in the past. And now, thanks to Edward and Mrs. Jennings, she'd be able to get on with her life.

"I really don't want to elaborate on my behavior," Natalie said. "Except to say that I'm terribly sorry if I caused either one of you any pain. I was faithful to you while we were engaged, Edward."

"Then the damage is not irreparable," Mrs. Jennings said, watching her shrewdly.

"But your friends and family, your reputation," Natalie murmured. "I can't possibly—"

"We haven't told anyone yet," Edward said.

Natalie gasped, staring at her fiancé. He looked so calm, so indifferent, effectively hiding his feelings behind a stony facade. He was a handsome man, although he rarely smiled. "You haven't officially called off the wedding yet?" she asked. Then she winced. "Oh, dear, I suppose I'm responsible for doing that, aren't I?"

Edward straightened in his chair. "I've decided to forgive you, Natalie. We all have our moments of doubt. And I know I can be...disinterested at times."

Natalie swallowed hard, astonished by Edward's admission. "Yes, you can."

"And I'd like to apologize for that. I hope to change. And I don't blame you for finding...solace in the arms of another man."

"Edward, it was more than just—"

"We don't need to hear the details," Mrs. Jennings said, sighing dramatically. "I'm sure we all know what happened. And it doesn't matter."

''We've both made mistakes,'' Edward said. ''We can put that in the past.''

''Then you can forgive me?''

''Yes,'' Edward said, pushing himself to his feet. ''I'll expect you at the church on Saturday, Natalie. Please don't be late.''

Natalie stared at him, aghast. ''The church? You want to go through with the wedding?'' Was he serious? Could he really forgive her so easily?

''That is why you asked to speak to me, isn't it? You wanted to salvage our wedding plans. Well, I've agreed. You made a mistake, I've forgiven you and we can go on as if nothing happened.''

''No, I—'' She stopped short. If he was willing to begin again, she should at least consider his offer. ''I had hoped we might...'' She paused. ''I never expected...'' She took a deep breath. ''I'll have to think about this. I'm grateful to you for your forgiveness, but—''

''Where the hell is her office?'' The shout echoed through the hallway outside of Natalie's door. She recognized the voice immediately and it sent a shiver of apprehension down her spine. Chase. She'd known that sooner or later he'd get tired of waiting. She just hadn't expected to confront him in the presence of Edward and his mother.

John Donnelly's voice joined the fray outside and then her door burst open. Natalie's heart leaped at the sight of Chase, his vivid green eyes, his thick hair combed by his fingers. He looked like he had that day they'd spent in bed—only now he had clothes on. Slowly, she stood and their gazes met.

"I've been waiting for you to call," he said, a frown creasing his forehead. "Dammit, Nat, it's been three days! Do you have any idea how worried I've been?"

Natalie glanced at Edward and his mother, and Chase realized that they weren't alone in her office. "What are they doing here?"

"We were just discussing the wedding," Natalie said.

Chase's jaw tightened. "What wedding?"

Natalie cleared her throat and gathered her resolve. "Edward, Mrs. Jennings, thank you for coming and for your forgiveness. But right now, I need to speak with Chase alone. If you'll excuse us?"

They both stood, then walked past Chase to the door, Mrs. Jennings shooting him a venomous glare and Edward merely sniffing in disgust. Chase looked like he was ready to punch Edward in the nose, but he managed to control himself.

When mother and son had finally taken their leave, Chase turned back to Natalie. "That was him? That was the man you were going to marry, that pompous, self-righteous bluenose? God, Natalie, what did you ever see in a guy like that?"

Natalie tipped her chin up defensively. "Edward and I care for each other. We're more suited than you and I are."

"That's not true," Chase replied.

She drew a long breath, gathering her resolve. "Edward has forgiven me for my...I don't know what to call it. A fling? It turns out that he takes partial blame for my insecurities. And now that we've straightened things out, we can go on with our lives as if nothing happened."

"But something did happen, Natalie. We fell in love."

"No. We shared a brief infatuation. And that was only because I thought we were destined to be together."

"I still believe we are, Natalie. I want you to marry me."

"I—I can't. I'm going to marry Edward as I planned."

Chase cursed, then shoved one of her office chairs aside as he stalked toward her desk. He placed his palms on the smooth wood surface and stared deeply into her eyes. "Tell me this is all a silly joke, Nat. Tell me you're not serious about going back to Edward."

Her gaze dropped to her hands, folded in front of her. "Your grandmother came to see me last night. We had a very nice talk. And when she dropped me off at Lydia's, she told me I would dream about my wedding that night. And I did. As clear as could be, I saw my wedding. And do you know who was waiting for me at the end of the aisle?" She paused, then looked up at him. "Edward."

Chase laughed harshly. "Why do you believe that vision and not mine?" he asked.

Natalie took a deep breath and let it out slowly. "Because my dream made more sense than yours."

Chase studied her for a long time, his gaze probing hers. "It's not about dreams and visions and destiny, is it? It all comes down to one thing. You're afraid."

"I don't know what you mean."

"You're afraid to love me. That's why you're willing to settle for a loveless marriage with Jennings. You're afraid that if you love, you'll be abandoned, the same way you were abandoned by your parents."

Again Natalie tipped her chin up. "That's ridiculous."

He shook his head slowly. "No, it's not. It's all very simple, Nat. You won't let yourself love me because you're afraid I might leave you."

She bit her lip, the truth of his words slowly sinking in. "I—I'm going back to Edward. I'm going to marry him. And nothing you say is going to change my mind."

He sighed in frustration, then bent his head. Natalie reached out to touch his cheek, but he backed away, anger flooding his handsome features. "Don't," he warned. "I can't accept this."

"Don't you see, Chase? None of this was ever meant to happen. We had a wonderful time, but that wasn't really me you were with. That was someone pretending to be irresponsible and impetuous."

Chase shook his head. "That's not true, Natalie. When we were in each other's arms, making love, I was making love to you. The real you. The warm, witty, wonderful woman that I met that first day in the elevator. I don't give a damn about the dream and I can live with your fears. The plain and simple fact is that I love you. And I want to marry you. We can work this out, I promise.''

''We don't know each other, Chase.''

''I know enough to know that I can't live without you.''

''Yes, you can. And I can live without you.'' Natalie slowly circled the desk and walked to the door. She pulled it open. ''I've made up my mind, Chase. Nothing you can say will change it. I'd like you to leave.''

He pushed away from the desk and faced her. ''Don't do this to us, Nat.''

''Please,'' she said, her voice barely a whisper. ''This is what I want.''

He raked his hands through his hair and cursed softly, then started toward her. She thought he was going to walk out without another word. But as he passed, his arm snaked around her waist and he yanked her up against his body. In the blink of an eye, his mouth was on hers, hard and demanding, filled with all the frustration she knew he felt.

Her knees went soft and desire welled up from her core, setting her nerves on fire. She returned his kiss, wrapping her arms around his neck as his tongue plundered her mouth. And then, as suddenly as he had drawn her into his arms, he pushed her away. Natalie looked up into eyes now as cold as ice.

''Remember this moment, sweetheart. Remember how I make you feel. And when you're lying next to your husband in bed, a passionless shadow of the woman you could have been, maybe you'll realize that you made a mistake.''

He turned and walked out of her office, out of her life.

Chapter Seven

NATALIE HAD FALLEN ASLEEP to the sound of rain, and when she woke up to the blare of her clock radio, it was still raining.

"Well, that nor'easter we told you about yesterday is here!" the DJ crowed. "Our weather gurus tell us that as much as three inches of rain has fallen in the greater Boston area, and it looks like we'll be getting some more because this baby is sticking around for a while. For now, all I can do is keep singin' in the rain here on Boston's number one rock 'n' roll station! Hey, if you can't stand my voice, how about a little Eric Clapton and 'Let It Rain.'"

She rubbed her eyes, slapped at the radio to shut it off, then stared up at the ornate ceiling of her bedroom in the Birch Street house. Rain on her wedding day. Though she didn't believe in omens, she was at least hoping that the weather would provide a suitable start to her married life.

Of course, Mother Jennings would be beside herself. How dare the weather put a damper on her son's big day? After everything the woman had been through in the last week, Natalie wouldn't be surprised if the storm sent her future mother-in-law right over the edge. That's all she had talked about at the rehearsal dinner last night, and Natalie was certain it would be the topic of endless breakfast conversation at the Jenningses' mansion. No doubt Edward's mother would find a way to blame it all on Natalie.

She glanced over at the clock on the bedside table. It was only 7:00 a.m. The hairdresser was coming at ten, and Lydia would be by to help her dress before noon. The two sisters would drive to the church together in a chauffeured limousine and arrive at precisely 12:50 p.m.

Natalie groaned and pulled the covers up to her chin. She wondered what would happen if she decided to arrive at 12:55 or even 1:00. Suddenly, she didn't feel like playing by the rules. In fact, she was beginning to hate all the rules— *Smile, dear. Be sure you talk to every guest. Thank-you notes must be sent within a week. Chin up, you're a Jennings now.*

Perhaps she should call Lydia and ask her to bring along her purple hair dye. What would Mrs. Jennings say to a nice streak of color beneath Natalie's veil? What would the guests say? She closed her eyes and smiled.

Chase would love it. He seemed to delight when she showed the smallest hint of impetuous behavior. She could jump naked into a vat of purple dye and he'd jump in beside her. In Natalie's mind an image of Chase flashed—of him lying in his bed, long limbed and leanly muscled. A tiny thrill shot through her and her breath caught in her throat.

It had been wonderful between them. Though she had tried to put the memories of their lovemaking aside, it was no use. They would be with her all the days of her marriage to Edward. But Natalie couldn't believe she was the only woman who had started married life carrying a torch for another man. Over time, the memories would fade.

She had made the right decision. Maybe she was afraid to love, but that didn't mean she couldn't have a happy marriage. Edward was a stable and dependable man—and he had been more attentive to her needs over the past few days. And he took his responsibilities seriously. She would never have to worry about him walking out on her.

Could she say the same for Chase? A man who lived his life footloose and fancy-free? He'd met her in an elevator and pursued her until she broke her engagement to another man. What would stop him from repeating the same impulsive behavior again—only this time with a more beautiful and available woman? Love was all fine and good, but she couldn't trust it.

Snuggling under the covers, she closed her eyes and tried to catch another hour of sleep. But thoughts of Chase refused to leave her head. She saw him behind the wheel of his car, wind blowing through his thick, dark hair. She saw him on his boat, in front of his house, and over and over again, in his bed, the sheets twisted around his naked body.

Cursing, Natalie sat up and shook the images from her mind. Then she scrambled out of bed and grabbed a silk dressing gown from the chair. She would need to find something else to occupy her thoughts. She'd write thank-you notes, a task guaranteed to numb her brain.

As she hurried down the stairs, the doorbell rang. Natalie stopped, her hand clutching the banister. She said a silent prayer, hoping that Mother Jennings hadn't decided on an unannounced visit. Perhaps Lydia had decided to come early. Or maybe another wedding gift was being delivered.

With a sigh, Natalie opened the door. Standing on the other side was the last person she expected to see on her wedding day. "Chase." The breath left her body and her heart stopped beating.

His hair was wet from the driving rain and moisture gleamed on the smooth planes and angles of his face. She wanted to reach out and brush the tiny droplets from his thick lashes, but she clenched her fists at her side.

For a long time they stared at each other silently, but she saw the emotion in his eyes, emotion he didn't attempt to hide. "What are you doing here?" she finally asked.

"I brought you a wedding gift." His voice was low and warm, the voice she'd heard over and over again in her dreams, the same voice that had called out her name at the height of his passion.

He held up a beautifully wrapped package, small enough to fit in the palm of his hand. Numbly, she took it from him and forced an appreciative smile. "That's very kind. You—you didn't have to do that."

"I wanted to. And I wanted the chance to tell you that I don't regret what happened between us."

"I don't either," Natalie said.

He reached out to touch her, then pulled his hand

back, cursing beneath his breath. ''All I want is for you to be happy.''

She stared down at the gift, toying at the satin ribbon with trembling fingers. ''What about you?''

Chase shrugged. ''I'll survive. I've decided to take a trip. My boat is in the water and I'm going to leave once the weather clears.''

The finality of their parting suddenly hit her. He'd be gone, out of reach, so far away that the connection between them would be irrevocably broken. ''Where will you go?''

''I don't have a plan. I'll just see where the wind takes me.''

She glanced up at him. ''I guess this is goodbye, then.''

He nodded, his gaze fixed on her face, studying her intently. She could see the indecision in his eyes and she wasn't sure that he could bring himself to turn and walk away. Lord knows, she couldn't. Every instinct told her to step into his arms and hold on tight. But she'd made her decision and she couldn't go back.

''You're sure about this?'' he asked, giving her one last chance.

Natalie nodded, biting on her lip to keep the wrong words from tumbling out.

Chase shrugged again and then smiled at her one last time before he turned and walked down the front steps. Natalie clutched the edge of the door with a white-knuckled hand, fighting the urge to call him back. She watched as he got into his car and started the engine, kept watching as he drove away and disappeared into the rain. He never looked back.

She stood in the doorway for a long time, waiting for him to return, the damp wind buffeting her icy skin. When she couldn't stand the cold any longer, she stepped back and shut the door. As the latch clicked, she felt a door close deep in her heart, putting an end to all they had shared.

Natalie wandered over to the stairs, then sat down on the bottom step, Chase's gift still clutched in her hand. Without thinking, she tugged at the satin ribbon and tore off the pretty paper. Inside the box, she found a small leather case, and inside that, a delicate antique compass, so small she could hold it in her fist.

She turned the compass over, wondering why Chase had chosen such an odd gift. And then she knew. Engraved on the back were the words she'd come to depend on in their short time together.

Anytime. Anywhere.

Tears pushed at the corners of her eyes and she pressed the gift to her heart. She found solace in the knowledge that he'd always be there, just beyond the horizon, waiting for her to call his name. Their connection would never be broken, not by marriage or time or endless seas. He would always have a special place in her heart, for he was the only man she would ever love.

''NATALIE, it's almost time to go. With this rain, we're going to have to leave a little earlier.''

Natalie glanced over her shoulder at Lydia, then

turned back to stare at her reflection in the mirror above her dresser. The rain drummed on the windowpanes, incessant and numbing. "Don't worry. They won't start the wedding without the bride."

She carefully straightened her veil, then ran her fingers along the shawl collar of her gown. She could feel the compass, cool and smooth, where she'd tucked it between her breasts. *Something old,* she thought to herself, plucking at the netting that cascaded over her shoulders.

Yards and yards of silk shantung rustled around her legs, and she could barely breathe in the tight bodice of her wedding dress. But she didn't want to breathe. She didn't want to think. All she wanted was to get this day over with and get on with her life.

A wedding was supposed to be the beginning of a dream, but to her, it seemed like the end, the last page in a beautiful love story. She pressed her hand to her gown, touching the compass. In some strange way, Chase's gift gave her comfort, the courage to live with the choices she had made.

"Natalie?"

She slowly turned and faced her sister, a melancholy smile touching her lips. "You look so pretty, Lydia. Like a princess. Remember when we were little, after Mom and Dad died? We used to lie in bed and pretend that we were both princesses, kidnapped from the palace as little babies and forced to live as orphans."

"Waiting for the day that the king and queen would find us and rescue us," Lydia continued. "There would be a big celebration in the kingdom and we would wear beautiful gowns and diamond tiaras."

"And we would both marry handsome princes and live happily ever after."

Lydia fell silent, her eyes searching Natalie's as if she were trying to read her thoughts. She drew a deep breath and then let it out. "Are you sure about this, Nat? It's not too late to back out."

"Why does everyone keep asking me if I'm sure? First Chase and now you. I made my decision and that's all there is to it."

Lydia arched her eyebrow. "Chase? You've seen him?"

"He stopped by earlier this morning to drop off a gift. It's all right. Everything's fine. He understands."

"Then maybe he can explain it to me," Lydia grumbled.

Natalie pasted a bright smile on her face and made a slow turn. "How do I look?"

Lydia bit her lip, tears welling in her eyes. "Like a princess." She brushed at her cheeks, then laughed. "We'd better go before I dissolve into puddles. The driver is waiting downstairs."

"You go," Natalie said, her voice calm and even.

A frown settled on Lydia's face. "What do you mean?"

"Go ahead. I'm not quite ready yet. I'll take my own car."

"Natalie, you can't drive yourself to your own wedding. Not in this weather."

Natalie reached out and took Lydia's hand. "I'll be

all right. Just go ahead and keep the guests—and the groom's mother—from getting restless. I need a few more minutes to myself."

"Do you think he'll come?" Lydia asked.

"Who?" Natalie knew exactly who Lydia meant, but she couldn't bring herself to acknowledge the hope that her sister's words brought. Maybe he would come. Maybe it would be like her childhood dreams—a prince on a white horse riding to her rescue.

"Is that why you want to wait? Do you think he'll come back?"

Natalie shook her head. Wanting it would not make it happen. They had said their goodbyes. "He's gone. For good. And he won't be back. I just need some time alone."

Reluctantly, Lydia nodded, then walked out of the room. Natalie turned to the mirror, staring at her reflection, at the stranger that looked back at her. She wasn't sure how long she stood there; she didn't really care. She waited until she could wait no longer. Then she turned and walked out of the room.

The driving rain had turned into a deluge; sheets of water fell from the gray sky, buffeted by gusty winds. Thunder rumbled in the distance and a flash of lightning split the sky. Natalie grabbed an umbrella and scooped up the skirt of her gown in her arms, then hurried to her car, parked under the port cochere. Rain spattered the silk and wilted her veil and she cursed her decision to forgo the limousine.

Wedging herself and her gown behind the wheel was much harder than she'd ever imagined. By the time she reached the church, she'd be a mass of wrinkles. And she could already feel her hair beginning to droop. So this wouldn't be the perfect day. But then, she didn't expect a perfect marriage, either.

She swung the car out of the drive, fighting her veil and the voluminous skirt that made finding the brake and accelerator close to impossible. The church was only ten blocks away, but the streets were unrecognizable through the rain that washed over her windshield. The wipers slapped an irritating rhythm, but were useless against the downpour.

Natalie felt the car drift and realized that she'd hit a huge puddle. Water flew up hitting the underside with a dull thud. She traveled only a few yards farther before the engine died.

Leaning back, she closed her eyes. "Maybe this is destiny," she murmured, listening to the rain drum on the hood of the car. "Maybe I'm not meant to get to the church." She shook her head, then reached for the ignition. "If I'm not meant to marry Edward, the car won't start."

The engine roared to life, and Natalie slowly maneuvered through the water. The next intersection was blocked by more flooding and she was forced to take a detour. As she drove on, nearly every street was blocked by water or police cars or drivers with stalled engines. She was running out of options and wondered if she'd ever find her way to the church.

"If the next intersection is closed, then I'm going to turn back. This is a sign. I'm not supposed to marry Edward." But the next intersection wasn't blocked and she turned toward the church, her heart pounding in time to the wipers.

A few moments later, the church appeared, the steeple stark against the pewter sky. It seemed as though the rain was beginning to abate. Natalie pulled the car into a spot directly in front of the doors. Through the foggy windows, she could see Edward and his mother standing in the entryway. They waved to her, but neither ventured beyond the threshold.

Suddenly, the skies opened up and water poured from the heavens. There would be no way to make it into the church without getting completely drenched in the process. Natalie gripped the steering wheel and bent her head. "Why is this happening? What am I supposed to do?"

Cursing, she grabbed her umbrella. If destiny was going to play a hand in her wedding day, then it better get off its butt and give her a sign. "If I'm not meant to marry Edward, may lightning strike the steeple of this church." She waited and listened as thunder rumbled, but lightning didn't bolt from the sky.

Gathering up her skirt, she shoved at the car door and popped open her umbrella. Natalie ran toward the entrance, dodging puddles and squinting against the downpour. By the time she reached Edward and his mother, her hem was soaked and her feet squished inside of her shoes.

"You're fifteen minutes late," Edward said, his jaw tight. "What were you thinking?"

Mother Jennings's hands plucked at Natalie's gown.

"My God, you're a mess. The pictures will be ruined. I'm humiliated. Look at you!"

Natalie shook out her skirt, then nodded to the organist, who loitered on the stairs to the choir loft. "I'm fine," she called. "We can start now."

With a sound of disgust, Mother Jennings grabbed Edward's arm and hustled him toward the sanctuary. She quickly took her place in the front pew, then turned to look back down the aisle.

Lydia appeared moments later, their bouquets clutched in her hands, her face lined with worry. "Are you all right? Good grief, Nat, I thought you were gone for good. Edward was ready to send the guests home, and Mother Jennings looked like she was about to throttle me."

"I'm fine," Natalie said, taking her flowers. The processional sounded from inside the church and she took a deep breath and nodded to her sister. "Go ahead. It's all right. Really."

Reluctantly, Lydia stepped through the door, glancing over her shoulder once more to be certain that Natalie was planning to follow.

When Lydia was the proper distance ahead, Natalie pasted a smile on her face and began the long march toward her future. The guests stood as she entered, and she saw Edward at the end of the aisle, a perturbed expression on his face.

Her shoes still squished beneath her waterlogged skirts, and a strand of wet hair hung over her eyes, tickling her nose. She felt like the main attraction at a bizarre circus, what with water dripping down her face, undoubtedly causing her mascara to run. A giggle burst from her throat, surprising guests on either side of the aisle. Before long, she could barely contain herself, forcing back laughter at her ridiculous situation.

Halfway up the aisle, Natalie stopped, unable to take another step. She looked at Edward and then at Mother Jennings, and then took a slow survey of the guests. Her life, her future, suddenly became crystal clear. ''Oh, to hell with it,'' she muttered, wiping her wet nose with the sleeve of her dress. ''What am I afraid of?''

A low murmur grew around her as the procession continued but she didn't. Lydia stopped and turned around, confused by the commotion. She sent Natalie an encouraging look, but Natalie shook her head and shrugged.

A tiny smile curled Lydia's lips. ''Go!'' she shouted.

Mother Jennings stepped forward, fanning her face with her program. She started toward Natalie. Natalie looked at her sister once more, laughed, then scooped up her skirts and spun around, tossing her bouquet aside.

Her feet nearly flew as she ran down the aisle. The murmur of the guests became an uproar, and she heard Edward and Mother Jennings shout her name. Shoving open the front doors of the church, she hurried down the steps, praying that she hadn't locked the keys in the car.

She'd nearly reached the street when she looked up

and saw Chase's Porsche parked next to her vehicle. Natalie froze, rain pouring down on her, drenching her to the skin. Then the passenger door opened and Chase leaned across the seat. She bent down and looked at him.

"Need a ride?" he asked, a smile twitching the corners of his mouth.

"Yes, I think I do."

Natalie stuffed herself and her wedding gown into the Porsche, battling the yards of silk and tulle that stood between them. Finally, she pushed her veil aside and found him staring at her, a bemused expression on his face. She sighed. "You came for me."

Chase chuckled, then bent closer and brushed a kiss on her moist lips. "Anytime. Anywhere."

A STIFF BREEZE FLUTTERED the sails of the *Summer Day* as the boat sliced through the choppy water. Sand Harbor grew smaller on the horizon and Chase checked the compass, then steered the boat toward the southeast and the Cape Cod Canal. The rain had stopped somewhere between the church and the marina. Sun filled the sky and the air had warmed to a balmy temperature, though the weatherman was predicting scattered storms for the next few days.

In Chase's mind, there had never been a more glorious spring afternoon. His gaze came back to the bow of the boat where Natalie stood, her wedding dress blowing and billowing around her body, her veil obscuring her face. She held tight to the jib stay and stared out at the rough waters of Cape Cod Bay as the spray shot up from the prow.

He wanted to go to her, to draw her into his arms and tell her that she'd made the right decision. But she would have to discover that on her own, in her own time. He didn't know how long it would take for all her fears and insecurities to vanish, but he was willing to wait. He loved her and there would never be another woman for him.

Chase watched her for a long time, recalling the dream that had brought them together just a few weeks ago. And then, as if part of that dream, Natalie turned around and smiled at him, brushing at her flyaway veil with her hand. "Where are we going?" she called over the sound of the water rushing past the hull.

"Wherever the wind takes us!" he replied. "We'll stick close to shore in case the weather kicks up again. And we'll spend the evening somewhere along Buzzards Bay."

She nodded, then smiled. The sun streaming over his shoulder bathed her in light. He'd never seen anything more beautiful. His Natalie, his beautiful, sweet Natalie. They'd come to the boat right from the church, Chase anxious to get her out on the water where she couldn't change her mind—and where Edward couldn't find her.

The boat hit a wave and spray shot up over the prow, falling on her head. She waved at him playfully, then laughed. He watched in delight as she reached up and pulled off her veil, and with a shout, tossed it overboard. The net caught the breeze and floated like a cloud. They watched it drift in the spill of wind from the sail before it dropped to the surface of the water.

"Just like my dream," she called with a laugh. "The wind and the veil. That was in my wedding dream."

Natalie moved toward him, her shoeless feet peeking out from beneath her gown. Then she stopped and grabbed hold of the shroud, balancing herself against the sway of the boat. Slowly, she reached behind her and unzipped her dress, sending him a tantalizing smile. Her dream had come true and now his had come to life. Chase could only stare as she stepped out of her gown and kicked it over the side of the boat.

She was left in lacy scraps of underwear—a pretty bra and panties, a garter belt and white stockings. With deliberate care, she undid the garters and slid the stockings over her ankles. Chase groaned, but he couldn't look away, transfixed by desire. His knuckles turned white as he clutched the wheel of the boat.

One by one, the stockings fluttered over the side, followed by the garter belt. Chase felt himself growing hard. She took a few more steps toward him, and with a soft curse, he flipped on the autopilot, letting the boat steer itself. In three quick steps he was standing below her, his hands out to help her into the cockpit.

With a coy look, she tumbled into his arms, all soft flesh and sweet curves. He kissed her long and deep, their tongues tangling, bodies melding, her skin cool against his palms. She shivered and he pulled back and looked into her eyes.

"Cold?"

"Freezing," Natalie murmured. "But you can warm me up."

Chase kissed the tip of her nose. "What am I going to do with you? Such a wanton woman. You threw all your clothes overboard."

Natalie's eyes grew wide. "You do have something for me to wear, don't you?"

He shook his head. "Nope. Besides, I like what you have on. The perfect wardrobe for a first mate."

"Chase! I can't sail to paradise without any clothes."

"Is that where we're going, then? Paradise?"

She wriggled in his arms, then reached down and pulled something from between her breasts. It was his compass—her compass. Natalie held it up to him and he took it from her fingers. "I guess you did come prepared."

She pressed against him and he gathered her closer, wrapping his jacket and his arms around her. "I want to live life," she said. "I want every day to be an adventure. I don't want to be frightened of what's waiting beyond the horizon. And I don't want to settle for anything less than true love."

"What about your career?"

"I was thinking that I'd be happy never to walk into that building again."

Chase chuckled. "And I was thinking that maybe I should settle down. I've got an office at Donnelly Enterprises. Maybe I should learn to use it."

Natalie looked up at him and placed her palm on his cheek. "We don't have to decide right now. Let's just keep sailing. Let's find an island where we can be alone, where we can run naked on the beach and make love in the sand."

"A place with a tiny, whitewashed church where we can get married."

"Paradise," she said.

Chase smiled and kissed her. He wanted nothing more than this—the woman he loved standing next to him, the wind at his back and the endless horizon in front of them. Wherever they roamed, they would always have each other. For he had made a dream come true and he held paradise in his arms.